CHILD'S PLAY
THE BREAD OF TIME TO COME

By the same author

JOHNNO
AN IMAGINARY LIFE
THE YEAR OF THE FOXES AND OTHER POEMS

CHILD'S PLAY

THE BREAD OF TIME TO COME

Two Novellas by

DAVID MALOUF

GEORGE BRAZILLER
NEW YORK

First published in the United States in 1981 by George Braziller, Inc.

For information address the publisher:
George Braziller, Inc.
60 Madison Avenue
New York, NY 10010

Library of Congress Cataloging in Publication Data

Malouf, David, 1934–
Child's play.

I. Malouf, David, 1934– . Bread of
time to come. 1981 II. Title
PR9619.3.M265A15 1982 823 81-21696
ISBN 0-8076-1351-7 AACR2

Printed in the United States of America
First paperback edition, 1994

CHILD'S PLAY

1

One afternoon at the end of autumn, during my last time at home with my father – a farewell visit is how I thought of it, though with any luck it might not be – I walked alone to an abandoned farmhouse on the other side of the stream that was up for sale at last and which I thought I might make a bid for; a way perhaps of ensuring the future would exist by setting my hand to an official document, a ninety-nine year lease.

I had known the place as a child and always loved it. It stands on a slight rise looking back into the valley, an unusual view that suggests that before there was a farm there the site might have had other, darker uses. Two ancient cherry-trees grow hard against the wall, there are pears, apples, half-a-dozen stunted olives; but what always attracted me to the place were the markings on its marble doorstep. A single stone, deep sunk and hollowed with footsteps, it might once, my father suggested, have been an Etruscan altar.

It was a clear day without cloud and unseasonably warm, which I took to be, on the sky's part, a special dispensation in my favour, a kind of blessing. I undressed, waded waist deep in the icy stream, stretched out afterwards on the gravel shore till I was dry enough to resume my clothes, and began the climb uphill, through thickets of tangled broom and deep, thickset brambles. It took nearly an hour.

The doorstep was smaller than I had remembered, but the markings, two rows of them, were still there, cut so deep you could read them with your fingers, and I had the sudden clear recollection in doing so in the bright sunlight of the first time I had tried it as a child. The script, my father insisted, was indecipherable. But I had been convinced that the stone stood in a unique relationship to me and that if I shut my eyes and traced the letters with my fingers the darkness itself would reveal their meaning. The idea now made me smile. But I shut my eyes just the same and my fingers followed the grooves.

The key was where the agent said it would be, tucked into a crack between bricks. Slapping the big roan mare that had followed me up from the gate and stood nuzzling my palm, I stepped through into the ground-floor stall. The horse, smelling apples, poked her soft nose in after me.

I had come here often as a child – the place had been deserted for as long as I could remember – but only in summer when the stream was low enough to be crossed dry-shod. Exploring the high rooms had been one of my first adventures. Then later, as a lonely adolescent, I had come to read or daydream and to try, once again, with pen and paper, to solve the mystery of the Etruscan writing. There were two rooms overhead and an attic. Down below a feeding trough ran the length of the wall, with iron rings every metre or so where the cattle were tethered. There was straw, a bundle of kindling, the rich ammoniac smell of animal droppings.

I climbed the stairs. Several tiles were missing from the low-pitched roof and the woodwork, thin slats with tiles laid over them, showed through jagged gaps. The whole place was filled with a subdued autumn light that smelled intensely of apples, and in the second and larger room there was a spilled heap of them, wrinkled now and some of them wizzened to the size of walnuts but still deliciously sweet. I sat on the stone floor and munched away as if I hadn't eaten for a week, swallowing each apple whole, with real greed, then reaching for another. It was like biting into the sun. Down below the horse rubbed her flanks against the door jamb and stamped her foot on the earth.

Stretched out there in the familiar warmth under the roof, I felt transparent, filled with the breath of apples, biting into the future with absolute certainty now that it would be there, that I would survive my moment in the Piazza Sant' Agostino at P. and come back, and had no need to buy a house or do anything else to ensure it; that I would live for years, maybe for ever. It is difficult to explain these convictions without seeming foolish. They come to us from deep within, even if we receive the ambiguous message as a smell of apples, the gold of a late autumn afternoon, the taste, as we put it, of the sun.

But I should introduce myself.

I am twenty-nine years old and male. You will understand if I decline to give further particulars.

I am what the newspapers call a terrorist.

2

I have been living for nearly six weeks in a small, one-roomed apartment in the Palazzo C, just the sort of place – bedroom not much bigger than a cupboard, with a gasring for making coffee and a washbasin behind a screen – that lone students inhabit or workmen who have come in from the country.

There are a dozen of us on the fourth floor across the courtyard, all living in spaces created out of what must once have been servants' quarters, modest enough by the standards of an earlier century and now even further divided. It is a rats' nest.

Narrow stairways branch off into darkness at every turning. One of them must pass just behind my bed. I wake sometimes to hear footsteps, not twenty centimetres from my ear. It is as if someone were climbing, seven steps in all, into my skull. Another crosses the corner of the ceiling opposite. I have no clear picture of how the rooms and passageways in this part of the building are connected or where my room sits among them. I know the courtyard and a stone stairway leading out of it, a passage and its turnings, another stairway, another, a third even narrower than the last, then my door. It is better like that. Once I have reached the second floor I am beyond the point where I am likely to come face to face with anyone, either by night or by day.

The palace dates from the Renaissance and is still inhabited somewhere by the family of the duke. They must live in the *piano nobile* on the other side of the courtyard; I have on occasion seen lights in the big windows above the square. The second floor on that side is offices, lawyers for the most part with the usual medley of clients, and the third houses a language school whose students, full of noisy high spirits, crowd the vestibule, hang about in groups on the stairs and are endlessly passing in and out of the barred carriage-way.

All this traffic means that the main door, which is three metres high and of solid walnut, is never shut. It also means that those who pass in and out go largely unremarked by the two porters. There are so many different types: separated couples and petty criminals in three-piece suits on their way to consult the lawyers, Swedish, American and English girls, Brazilians, New Zealanders, Swiss, sometimes a half-dozen Egyptians or an African army or police corps looking uncomfortably out of place as civilians, foreign executives, airline pilots, hippies – all students of the two-week course at the language school.

A single terrorist of quiet habits and with no distinguishing marks, heavy hair neither long nor short, jeans and Levi jacket some months faded, tallish, middle to late twenties, would pass un-noticed among this gathering of the nations. Some of my neighbours on the fourth floor must be genuine workmen, but given that they too wear jeans and a Levi jacket, have moustaches, sideburns and are of quiet habits, they may equally be language students, or students of art or literature, or terrorists.

The courtyard is damp and all its walls are scarred and patched with damp. The arcades, closed off with ironwork screens of a depressing brutality and weight, are piled with firewood and broken stones, fragments of what must once have been noble decoration. The various classical deities, minus a flexed wrist or with the genitals amputated or half the face gone as in a stroke, rub shoulders with eagles, peacocks, cornucopias, flamelike finials, quartered shields and heraldic beasts both real and fabulous, urns, putti, wingless angels gone green with mould – an anthology, as it were, of our rarest follies and illusions.

The main staircase is barred with ironwork and never used. It bears a short chain, doubled, and a rusty padlock. All entrance to the apartments on the second and third floor, and to our wing at the rear, is by the same stone stairway in the corner of the yard.

I have seen lights in the windows at all levels in these side wings but have never met anyone on the stairway or glimpsed even a shadow in the various corridors.

Once, looking up briefly as I passed through the inner portal, I saw a hand watering a geranium pot and a puff of what must have been pipe smoke. On another occasion, late at night, I heard a thin male voice calling 'Lady, where are you Lady? Why won't you come to poppa? Poppa's lonely. Where are you?' I assume he was calling to one of the several cats, some wild, others no doubt domesticated, that stretch themselves on the warm flags of the courtyard or among the broken gods and putti behind the grills, and make their way precariously, between pots of geranium and petunia, from one side of the palace to the other, tracking the sun. On yet another occasion, turning the stairs at the second landing, I heard from a half-open door down one of the corridors, the sounds of a man and woman fighting. The woman uttered piercing screams, the man's voice murmured soft indistinguishable petitions, and the whole scrabbled din was punctuated by muffled thuds that must have been blows. Then before I was quite out of earshot, the whole episode concluded with the slamming of a door.

The room was found for me. I came straight to it from the station, having been in the city only once before, when my father brought me as a child to visit the museum. The name of the palace and the number of my room, with indications of how to find it, headed a list that includes four safe restaurants, four laundromats that are within easy walking distance (I never go to the same one twice) and three streets in different quarters where there are prostitutes.

All this is perfect. The palace, with its promiscuous entry and its world of obscure privacies, is cover. The city too is cover, crowded as it is at all times of the year with tourists, transient students of language, permanent students at the various art schools and technical colleges, and at the University. I am invisible here. I go out of my room at eight like any factory hand or office worker and return at dusk. In the evening I dine alone and go to a movie.

I am invisible. Just like everyone.

3

Our hideout as the newspapers would say (we call it an office) is in an apartment block on the other side of the river. I take two buses then go on foot for the last three hundred metres, through a maze of streets too narrow for traffic; under archways, down twisting lanes, across piazzas no bigger than a pocket handkerchief where women, in the pale sunlight of these April mornings, are already throwing buckets of water over the cobbles or setting up stalls with vegetables and cut flowers and men are at work delivering trays of pastry, crates of Fanta and Coca Cola and barrels of anchovies in brine.

Cut off as I have been over these last weeks from all the happenings of ordinary existence – I am by nature gregarious, not at all the brooding melancholic – I find the busy traffic of the quarter, with all its comings and goings, an endlessly engaging spectacle and take longer on my way to the office than the distance strictly demands. It makes up a little for the hours I spend alone in my barren room and for the narrow and impersonal view that is required by my work. Not that

I complain of this. It is necessary. It is a discipline. But it goes against the grain with me, and I find it easier to concentrate on pure facts if, for a few minutes before, I have been able to observe the confusion of voices and events that makes up the city and can retain, somewhere in the back of my head, the conviction that it is real and continuous and will be there to be re-entered when I am done. Each time I go down, with all the dossiers of my 'case' locked up in the filing cabinet behind me, is a rehearsal for my final re-emergence. For I have not relinquished life or given up even one of my high ambitions and hopes for the future. What I have given up is some weeks of my life and my legal innocence; and I have done so, I believe, in the name of that very life of the streets – ordinary, loud, richly confusing – that I shall go back to when my mission is complete.

Rich confusion is not its only quality, of course. There are patterns, and I find them sustaining. (Is my nature really conservative?)

I like for example to see the same children, at the same hour, making their way in noisy groups towards the primary schools across from the park; skipping along hand in hand, trudging with head lowered as they repeat some childish spell and try, without trying, not to step on the lines, dancing backward on their heels to call to a straggler. Their scrubbed faces shine. They have little satchels strapped to their backs, or carry brief-cases that are too big for them and drag their bodies awkwardly to one side. Bright blue pinafores cover their sweaters and slacks.

For all these weeks a team of plasterers has been at work on an old palazzo near my bus-stop, and usually, by the time I pass, they are already on the job, balanced high up on the iron scaffolding or on planks and ladders in the open rooms. They are a boisterous lot, forever shouting from room to room or calling into the street. Their heads are protected with linen caps, their overalls caked with plaster, and the youngest of them, the apprentice, is regularly covered from head to foot with the paint he has been mixing. I like to see them up there, busily swinging their brushes, joking and calling to one another, or pausing to watch a pretty girl pass in the street below, and have begun to reckon time by their progress up the side of the building and through its rooms, by the changing colours of what can be seen of the interior, all sparkling fresh with new paint and soon to be occupied. The work of these decorators, and the great corner palace itself, has become my private clock. I often consult it when I need to fix, in the otherwise featureless landscape of these weeks, some little event or movement of my own thoughts. *Ah yes,* I say, *that was before those rooms on the second floor had the gilt on their ceilings. Or was it after? Yes, after.*

Then there are the beggars, always the same ones; each quarter has its own.

An old woman bent almost double, who wears boots that are a size too large for her, has her own place near the paper stand. With one hand boldly extended and her face bent low to the pavement, she murmurs an incomprehensible litany. Further on a youth with a shaven head sits hunched against the wall with his face between his knees. An empty box lies on the pavement beside him, together with a placard describing his plight: he is blind and has neither family nor work. Passers-by, always the same ones, dip their hands in their pockets or turn delicately aside (the women) to examine their purse. They place coins in the outstretched palm, or leaning over, drop them very discreetly into the box.

All this is part of the fabric of things and is essential to its pattern. So too is the fat owner of the hardware shop, who stands in the doorway under the hanging pots, pans, broomsticks, and the tin and plastic buckets, with a black book in her hand, always the same one, which I assume is a bible and which when the sun is shining she sits reading on a three-legged stool. And the delivery vans with their various boys; and the early shoppers with their plastic bags printed with the names of local stores. It is against the accommodations, the collisions, the dense proximities of this street life, all its repeated details and events, confused but not without shape, that the simplicity of my own existence should be balanced, with its single event that must, for a while yet, be held back and kept separate and made to occupy my whole mind, but will at last become part of that rich confusion and may even change it a little. That this event is a killing is neither here nor there. Violence too has its place. There are brawls, road accidents, beatings-up behind closed doors; or one of my decorators might suddenly miss his footing and fall twenty metres from the scaffolding. There is death. The important thing is not to see the single event in isolation. Though in fact, for these weeks, that is just how I am required to see it. And that is why, for the sake of my own sanity, I have to spend a little time each day in the street.

But I should return to the facts.

Our office.

It is housed in an apartment block that presents the same faded appearance, crumbling plaster, patches of raw brick, as every other building in this older part of the city. At street level there is a showroom for bathroom fittings, on the first floor an architect's office; beyond that a dozen big, comfortable apartments. Ours bears the name *Rizzoli, G.* on a brass plate in the vestibule, and on another, larger and more elaborate, in the middle of the door.

Inside, what ought to be a family dwelling has been set up as office, library, information-bank and arsenal. It is all very cleverly and professionally arranged.

Five of us work here from half-past eight in the morning till seven at night, six days of the week. We work in the big main room of the apartment, which can be sealed off and defended from the corridor. We each have a desk facing the wall and a filing-cabinet, and we are always armed. It is strange to sit all day, as you might sit in the corner of a quiet library, bringing your mind to bear on a set of problems or giving it free range in the fields of the imagination, and to have always at your side the weight, the coldness (till it absorbs a little of your own body-heat) of a revolver; and even stranger to know that you might, at any moment, have to use it. We have all been trained to use weapons and could fight our way out of here should it become necessary; or at least hold off an attack till our records were destroyed. The presence of cold steel is a reminder of our vulnerability and keeps us alert. It also keeps us aware, during these quiet library days among the facts and photographs, of that hard moment to which they lead, when we will stand alone at last with the weapon naked in our hand.

One of the bedrooms is a library and information bank that contains, for example, lists of prospective victims, their names, their addresses and the first essentials for a study of their life and habits.

The other, though still set up as a sleeping place, with double-bed, dressing-table and lace curtains in the window, is our arsenal. The built-in wardrobe is stocked with hand-grenades, revolvers of various weights and calibres, repeating pistols, machine guns, anti-tank missiles, dynamite sticks and other devices for the manufacture of bombs, and a good supply of ammunition. But the bed is changed and slept in, there are cosmetics on the dressing table, clothes in the wardrobe: woollen suits neatly covered with clear plastic oversheets, summer dresses, scarves, and on a shelf at the bottom a whole row of sensible shoes and (a little incongruously one might think) a pair of coral-pink glossy leather sandals. We must assume that Signora or Signorina Rizzoli, Gina, has a real existence and lives here in the hours when we are away. Along with the usual mail, two popular magazines are delivered in her name every second

Thursday – the sort that are devoted to the lives of starlets and to international gossip, together with a parish newsletter.

She fascinates me this Signora Rizzoli, who sees that the kitchen is supplied with the makings of a good lunch and whose grey hairs I have examined in a hairbrush but who herself remains mysteriously invisible. By the time we appear in the morning she has already left. We just miss her; though only, I suspect, by minutes. Have we passed in the street below without recognizing one another? Or was the ignorance on one side only? Does she perhaps keep watch on us, our appearance, our times of arrival and departure, and file a report?

It is in the nature of things that I have no answer to these questions. I know nothing of the structure of our organization and its agencies, or the part that might be played in it by a Signora Rizzoli. I have been recruited for a special purpose and my ties with the organization involve a single event, after which I shall sever all connection with it and disappear. Signora Rizzoli, like so much else that occupies me here, both fascinates and eludes me.

Those coral pink sandals for instance. It is part of my failure to catch and hold her – a failure that rather pleases me, I find it reassuring – that those sandals cannot be fitted to what I already know of her life and interests. Sitting there at the bottom of the wardrobe among her sensible shoes they seem deliberately intended to mislead. What do they represent? A secret weakness, a lapse in taste, a lapse of character? Some fleeting image of herself in the window of a boutique that she was unable to resist and keeps shamefully hidden from view? I imagine Signora Rizzoli, when no one else is here, taking her coral-pink sandals from the wardrobe, strapping them to her small feet, and walking round the apartment as if it were a fashionable summer beach, deliberately stepping out of character and using the sandals, as she uses the two magazines and the parish weekly, to throw off the scent an imaginary policemen who might already have his eye on the dour, dark-suited language teacher. Or are the sensible shoes, the pink sandals, the magazines, the parish weekly and the Signora's role as language teacher all of a piece? And is it precisely this that makes her, from the organization's point of view, the perfect owner-occupier of an apartment that is being used by terrorists?

While we are at our desks in the workroom, between half-past eight and twelve-thirty, and again between half-past one and seven, we are forbidden to speak, and though this rule does not apply to the dining room, we do not speak there either.

This self-imposed isolation, as of a religious order, has no ideology behind it for which the religious life would be a proper model; it grows out of our work. There is something excessive, comic even, about those nineteenth-century anarchists who thought of themselves as a new breed of monks, above life and its ordinary conditions, abjuring alcohol and women and even denying themselves tobacco. We are workers, technologists; young people of good health, clear of spirit, and with no grudges, no phobias, no sense of personal injustice or injury, none of those psychological or physical defects that are so dear to the hearts of journalists and so comforting to their readers. If we keep to ourselves and eat in silence it is because we have, in our long hours at the desk, gone too deep into the future and stood too long, in imagination, in our lonely moment there, to indulge in small talk or the commonplaces of a social life. There are cells that are units, training together for a group event, a bank robbery or a raid on a rival organization. Others come together only out of administrative convenience and for mutual protection. Ours is of the second sort. We each have our separate commissions and work alone.

But there is another reason why we preserve a wary distance from one another and prefer to see no more than appears on the surface or can be guessed at from those little habits of behaviour and appearance that inevitably give one away.

What we bring to the office is a steely impersonality that belongs to our role as killers. It looks inviolable, and it must be so. It is a form of security. To open to others all that lies beyond the hard surface, the doubts, fears, hesitations, anxieties of the lonely individual, all the soft dark life within – those moments when, walking along in sunlight, you come suddenly to a full realization of what you have let yourself in for, the irreversible nightmare – would be to introduce an element that might entirely destroy us, since it is on a steady imperviousness to all this, to the need that grips you some days to speak out and share a moment of tenderness felt or poignantly recalled, an unimportant event out of a past that is dense with unimportant but memorable events, that our security is established. What makes us useful as killers is that we have no past. The crimes we are to commit have no continuity with us. Nothing in their geography, their politics, their psychology, leads back to what we are. To speak out and offer confidences, to exchange memories, would be entirely disruptive. So we say nothing, and of those others who make up the four remaining points of the pentagram I know only what I can see, or have picked up by intuition from what cannot, even with effort, be concealed.

Carla (it is not her real name, we all have code-names here) occupies the working-place behind me. She is a tall blond girl who wears expensive cardigans, tweed skirts, boots. She smokes incessantly with quick nervous movements like a non-smoker, sucking at the cigarette and pulling it quickly away from her mouth with a gesture that has to be carried through to arm's length, and when she laughs she shows all her teeth; it is as if she had convinced herself that laughing is good for the facial muscles and should be made the most of. She is the only one of us who looks a little, I think, like a fanatic.

When her face is in response she has a faintly disdainful air, as though there emanated from some object in her vicinity an odour of corruption that is just detectable to her finer nostrils. She is a perfectionist. I watch her lean over a page, and with an eraser held very precisely between thumb and fore-finger, remove an error. The tip of her tongue appears. The agent of her moral being, her tongue is very lively and pink; it moves with the eraser and is committed to silence. 'There,' she says, dealing gently with God, 'I have erased an error. I have erased one of *Your* errors. The page is blank again.' She lifts a strand of hair from her eyes and smiles with satisfaction, like a very competent twelve-year-old, but when she glances up and finds me looking her brow creases. I have caught her in a moment from the past.

At mealtimes she crumbles her bread nervously with her left hand and does not eat it – a habit I find un-nerving, I can't say why; and when she walks she strides. I think of her being pulled along at the end of a straining leash by some invisible hound. These are observations that may point to none of the conclusions I draw from them. Namely, that Clara is convent educated, country bred and a lapsed aristocrat. She is highly efficient in every way and cooks, when it is her turn, with the same swift sure movements with which she smokes, flips through file-cards and makes her way through a crowd. She is the one I would put my trust in if (it is one of those things we have to consider) there were a raid on the apartment and we had to shoot our way out.

I wonder sometimes about her *event.* I see her advancing through glass doors to a bank hold-up, her leather boots squeaking softly on the parquet floor. I imagine what it would be like to be an old man, full of the corruptions of thirty years in office, who looks up suddenly to find her there, tall, unsmiling, with a repeating pistol in her hand, one of our beautiful Scorpions, and recognizes, with what mixture I ask myself of terror, relief, a disturbed and gratifying sensuality, the cool angel of his extinction.

For some reason when we go dancing I never choose Carla as a partner.

The truth is that she intimidates me. What was she in her former life? A student of anthropology, the bored wife of a city lawyer, a make-up consultant for a beauty firm? She is twenty-eight or thirty and her right hand shows a band on the fourth finger where she previously wore a ring. Once she passed boldly, but fleetingly, through one of my dreams. I feel sometimes that her appearance there, and the glow she left on my senses, told me more of what she really is than all our hours of sitting side by side in the apartment, and more than I have been able to deduce from my observations of her behaviour. But that sort of knowledge is untranslatable. Does she, I wonder, detect the small changes it has made in my attitude to her? Far from leading to greater intimacy between us it has put me at a disadvantage. She seems, more than ever, a mystery that I will never solve.

Antonella is a South American, from Chile or Uruguay. She wears an embroidered cloak, but is really too short to carry it off, and is so full of energy that even when she is working, absorbed in her files, or brooding, with a glass screwed into her eye, over a strip of tiny photographs, she suggests a girl dancing, moving about in her secret self to some popular song that she is humming under her breath, or maybe whistling – I see her as a whistler. It is a notion so strong in my sense of her that I find myself being distracted by her singing, and am tempted at times to turn round in the absolute silence and say, 'Antonella, for heaven's sake, be quiet! I can't work for the racket you're making.' Even at the dinner-table she sits in something less than silence. Like a bottle that is bubbling and about to pop its cork.

She cannot be more than twenty. I think of her as the eldest of a family of three or four. She gives the impression of a girl who has just (I say just but it may be weeks ago) wished an exuberant farewell to smaller brothers and a sister, and is still full of the glow of their affection for her and their sorrow to see her gone; as if, perhaps, she had slipped in to kiss the youngest of them in the bath and in leaning over the tub got soap bubbles in her hair that have not yet evaporated. She dances well, cooks badly, and is efficient in everything to do with her work; mostly, one suspects, because she is naturally careless and has to watch herself. If any one of us were to indulge in a practical joke it would be Antonella – though I can't imagine what form it might take. Strangely enough, she and Carla, for all their difference, get on enormously well. We are forbidden to see one another outside, except for the special occasions when we go dancing, but inside the apartment, in all sorts of small ways, one feels them moving together; whereas we males, less sure of ourselves, practice a wary hostility.

I can understand this in Enzo's case. He is a natural leader who finds himself now in a situation where all that side of him is superfluous because no leader is required.

It is comic to watch Enzo struggle with himself, to see him exclude from our relations with one another everything that is strongest in him. Comic, but also endearing. (Why are men so much more transparent than women? Is it because so large a part of what we are has to be recognized and appreciated by others?) Enzo's dark good looks, his marvellous head of hair, which he cannot prevent himself from tossing, his air of being a swimming star or a skier out of season, his obvious appeal to women, his confidence in his own power and presence – these are difficult qualities to exclude, and one has the sense of their waiting there, a little impatiently, a little petulantly, to be called back into the room and given full play among us. His hostility to Arturo and me is less, I think, because of any threat we present to his supremacy than for the hurt he feels on behalf of his banished 'qualities'. As if otherwise we might fail to appreciate that equality has been established among us only because of his noble abnegation.

Arturo's hostility on the other hand is defensive. He is a stocky nineteen-year-old with a mop of tight, blondish curls, strong, hard-working, good-humoured and afraid of being ignored because of his youth. It makes him hard-mouthed and aggressive on occasion, and more boyish than ever.

Once, by some unlucky accident, I ran into him at a pornographic movie. He was fiercely embarrassed. Here we are training together in the technology of murder and he is embarrassed to be seen at a porno movie. Our eyes met and he blushed and looked away, as if somewhere behind me stood the respectable peasants of the village he comes from, all dressed in their Sunday suits, rattling their watch-chains and saying, 'But that's Ivo's boy. He's been watching a dirty movie.'

4

No, if there is to be an image for us, for our isolation here and the rigour and intensity of our training, it cannot be that of the monk. It is an outmoded notion that all disciplines which subdue the personal to a larger idea are religious.

The image I prefer is that of the sportsman, living day after day, in every nerve of his body, in every fibre of his will, with an *event*. There is something clean and healthy in that, some vision of open air and horizons that seems more appropriate to us than the pale recluse. And especially those sportsmen who train in groups but will, at the last moment, act alone. The giants of our epoch are those lone figures whose real antagonist is themselves, even when their 'self' takes the form of a glassy peak in the Himalayas or an ocean or a desert or a stretch of time to be endured out in the vastness of space. An early flier like Lindberg, for example, taxies off to cross the planet on a fixed route that can be plotted on a chart, to cover a known distance from one point, named and with a history, to another named point – Roosevelt Field Long Island to

Paris France – but is adventuring, in fact, into the pure space of himself. It is not distance or air currents or a mathematical equation of air-miles against fuel consumption that he is in competition with but his own capacity to endure solitude, to drive a big frame with heavy bones that demands to be horizontal, and blood that lies in pools or trickles through narrow channels, from one point in time to another that is still invisible beyond the furthest horizon.

So, there it is, the ideal. We are swimmers, skiers, long distance runners, test pilots, walkers in space.

I think especially of that marvellous Japanese who set out to ski down Everest, living for all the months of his training with the mountain itself in his imaginary sights; letting his body breathe with it, taking its strange light into him as the sun up there struck cold off snow steeps and jagged ridges, its planetary silence in his skull, its flamelike air ablaze on the surface of his skin, its outcrops and crevasses shockingly concealed under whatever snow-run he was making, even in easy practise on the softest home fields. Then, at the end of long months, the haul to his unusual starting-point – the summit, and the measuring by slow steps, one after the next, hour after hour, in breathlessness and extreme bodily fatigue, of every centimetre of what he will cover later in just a few ecstatic seconds; and behind him as he climbs, set up in reverence at every stopping-place, the little mirrors in which the mountain's spirit is caught and reflected, the great antagonist.

Slowly, day after day, in imagination, I am climbing

towards the *event*. At the moment when it takes place I shall be flying, tumbling, skiing down all the hours of my sitting here day after day, my papers and photographs and newspaper cuttings flashing past now in a continuous stream, too fast to be read, but every fact recognized, known and brought into focus in the high strange air, in the piercing light of it and of the little mirrors I have set up to catch and hold its spirit, the pure, accessible sky peak.

5

Spread out on the desk where I work are half a dozen photographs of the piazza at P., together with a detailed plan of its four cross-streets and the various entries and exits. By putting the plan and the photographs together I have developed a clear notion of the place, but it has gaps, and the gaps worry me.

When laid out in series the photographs make a complete three-hundred-and-sixty degree view.

On the western side of the piazza, the church of Sant' Agostino that gives its name to the square: early fourteenth century, with one unfinished tower. To the north, across a busy cross-street, the public gardens. Arcaded shopfronts to the east, below a nineteenth-century mock-Renaissance façade. Then a second cross-street, without traffic, and closing the square at the southern end, a fortified gothic palace.

The gaps are not in the physical picture that presents itself to me (which I have built up through long hours of fixing my attention on the photographs so that they form a continuity in my head) but arise, as one might predict, from the difference between knowing a place in your five senses, as a three-dimensional space in which you move and breathe (from having actually been there and experienced, for example, the relative difference between your own height and that of an unfinished tower) and a knowledge that has been arrived at by induction, in which every detail, however sharply observed and recorded, has bypassed the senses altogether. The gaps, I mean, are in myself.

The photographs themselves are very striking. They have been taken by one of our agents, a professional in this business. I imagine him posing as a tourist, standing there in the sunlit bowl of the square and making his seven shots, *snap, snap, snap,* in a perfect circle. It is into the shape of this make-believe tourist that I slip when I enter the square, and through his eyes that I see the place; which means that as far as my knowledge goes, the Piazza Sant' Agostino at P. exists entirely in its own space. Of P., a small provincial town of no particular distinction, I know only a single piazza, sunlit, pigeon-crowded, hanging in mid-air, and surrounded in my vision of it by perpetual fog.

This then is the scene of the crime, a place approached not by ordinary streets where families live and traffic moves, where things are made, bought and sold, consumed, broken, but by weeks of careful preparation. It is not a playground, this piazza, for teenage footballers, a crossing point to another part of the town, or a gathering place for young and old, but a stage-set awaiting events, and its appearance, after so many centuries, in the light of 'history'.

So then, let me take my imaginary walk around it, beginning with photograph number one.

What I have before me is the unfinished façade of the church, a clear expanse of golden plaster, roughened here and there with brickwork and broken by a rose window with six marble spokes and three ornamented doors.

The effect of roughness is exaggerated in the photograph because the sun is slanting in from the north-west, casting heavy shadows, and the same elongated shadows fall (I almost said flow, since they have the consistency of slow tar or lava) from the steps that lead down into the piazza from a platform that runs the whole length of the façade. There are four steps in all, and the platform, which is five or six metres wide, is of flagged stone. It provides, at this hour, a playing-space for a group of schoolboy footballers. They are wearing sweaters pushed up at the elbow, and their jackets can be seen in a pile on the steps, so I guess it is autumn or early spring, about four-thirty in the afternoon. Judging from the size of the pile there must be thirteen or fourteen of them.

The player closest to the camera is, of course, larger than the rest; his head and one shoulder are blurred. He is moving in fast to where the ball is rising towards him at thigh level. You can see its shadow on the wall.

Six other boys appear in various postures and at various distances from him, and several of them recur in later shots; but some of the players, one guesses, never appear at all, though they were clearly present all the time the square was being photographed. This is because our photographer, following his own needs, was moving in a continuous circle from right to left, while the football game, following the unpredictable flight of a ball and the players' attempts to place themselves in its path, was in violent progress all about him.

So here too is a gap. Several of the footballers, though they too were in the square, simply failed, in the disorderly bunching and shuffling of the game, to get recorded. They exist only in the gaps between shots, like the noise the players were making, their shouts of 'Here!', 'To me!', 'Faster!' which are also absent and represent a deficiency in the photographer's art.

So then, details.

I note the four steps and the width of the platform. Moving close in, using a glass, I note that the central door of the church, a fine bronze with monumental hinges, is permanently closed. A woman in black carrying two plastic bags has just emerged from the door to the south, scattering the shadows of a dozen pigeons across the façade. Another figure, having already descended the steps, is moving off (we see only her back) towards the cross-street. The door of the church is still swinging behind someone who has just entered, or is being pulled back by someone who has yet to emerge. No action, except from the footballers, at the north end of the façade, and the lintel over the north door, and the platform in front of it, are crusted with droppings. Only the south door is in use.

This is the door he will emerge from.

The crime will take place on the platform, or on one of the four steps leading down from it, on the south side of the square.

The second photograph shows just such a place. In this shot the old woman who has just emerged from the church is about to step down into the well of the square, and the woman whose back we saw in the previous photograph is in profile, but too far off to be clear. She is crossing the narrow street towards the gothic palace, her head turned to take account of an approaching cyclist.

The palace I call gothic has one large central gateway leading to a courtyard. No windows, but a loggia with six pointed arches about halfway up, then crenellations and a square tower with a pole. The street that leads away beyond it into the town is dark and narrow (the first of the two women seems to be moving towards it) and reveals nothing, either of itself or of what lies beyond, since it almost immediately makes a deep arc. No amount of peering or moving up close with the glass will take me further along that street, but I continue to stare at it, as if I could somehow, by sheer will-power, set the woman's stopped figure in motion and follow her round the curve.

A safe part of the square, this. Quiet. There is no post for observation (even the loggia is blind), nothing is happening. The end of the street is closed off with three bollards and a chain, so that the cyclist who is approaching (illegally it seems) will have to pass between one of the bollards and the palace wall.

It is the part of the square I feel most secure with. I

have become quite fond in a way of the cyclist (a fat man in a beret) and of the two women who have appeared at just this moment and are, for me, the familiars of this side of the piazza, enlivening its uneven flags with their presence. The one with the two plastic bags stoops with their weight. The other is also stooped, but the weight she carries is invisible. They must have been to vespers, or have slipped into the cool church to pray for a moment or to be alone in that still place with the spirits of the dead, a husband or a son lost in the war. It would please me – I mean I would find it a comfort – if they could be there at the time of the event; I have got used to them. Though in fact their faces are so unclear that I wouldn't recognize them if they did appear, and who knows what their habits are and what they are normally engaged in at this particular hour? (*Is* this the hour? Is that why the photographs have been taken at – I am guessing – between four-thirty and five in the afternoon?)

We move on past the palace to the intersection. Traffic approaches at right-angles here and turns west. There is a paperstand at the corner with a striped awning, then the bollards that close the street. More bollards and chains close the extension of the main street along the western edge of the piazza, and in front of them several motorinos are parked, some with the riders still astride, and more young people are strung out in the sunlight towards the middle of the square.

This is a social corner, you see that immediately. Strange the dynamics of the thing. The activity that begins here extends into the next photograph, which shows part of the arcaded shopping area, with more bikes and more young people milling around what appears to be a café or ice-cream parlour. Yes. Examined with the glass, several of these young people prove to be holding cones. One or two of the faces can be made out, especially that of a blond girl whose hair has come loose; she is laughing, throwing her head back, and trying to take the hair from her eyes while holding the ice-cream at such an angle that it is about to topple from the cone. But mostly the faces are a blur. The arcade behind the columns has canvas blinds. At this hour, and at this time of year, the blinds are rolled halfway up. Peering beneath them, again with the aid of a glass, you can make out shops: a café with two long windows, a shoeshop, and what seems from the sacks outside to be a store that sells grain.

The shop-fronts continue unbroken in the next photograph: another café more or less deserted, a window with curtain materials and cushions and at the corner a bank. But this photograph is utterly deserted and the lack of people affects its mood like a change of weather. Even when you put the photographs together and try to take in the whole western side of the square at a single sweep, the disjunction is unmistakable. It is as if one of the shots had been taken on a different day from the rest.

Everything about this view is depressing – the bank with its drawn curtains, the unfashionable café, the shop with curtain materials that nobody is looking at or wants to buy, the sense one has that the piazza slopes to the south (does it? Could one tell that from the lean of the motorinos or the stance of the girls?) and that its life is naturally drawn off in that direction. (Is it because of some inclination of the land itself, and its influence over the centuries, that only the south door of the church is in use?).

But I am haunted by another quality of this view that has nothing to do with absence of people or the fact that the westering sun sets its buildings in deep shadow, flattening their projections and blurring their hard lines.

Turning away from the event, which will have taken place at the south end of the platform – or if more than one shot is needed, on the steps – it is this view that will confront me as I run, my ears filled with the echo of the shots and the cries of bystanders, to where the car will be waiting at the corner beyond the bank. The mood of this photograph belongs not to the time when it was taken but to the moment immediately after the killing. It lacks people because they have been drawn to the commotion opposite. The square has naturally emptied towards the south, and I alone am running in the other direction.

For all its lack of interesting detail, this is the view that has most to reveal. It tells me what I shall see – and perhaps even how I shall feel – in the moments after the crime. It is a photograph of the future.

The remaining views, showing the north side of the square, seem altogether less important; everything significant, as we have seen, happens at the other end. But it would be intolerable to have a square in your head that was open to the unknown on one whole side.

Photographs six and seven fit neatly together to make a public garden, which from the disposition of the trees, all regularly planted and clipped, must be laid out in formal walks, maybe even with fountains and a pond. A gravel path runs up the centre with an equestrian statue at the point where it is crossed by side paths. The statue is of stone, and the horse has been caught in its progress out of the nineteenth century towards the wide street that runs along the north side of the square, which must, to judge from the traffic, be one of the city's major thoroughfares. (When I reach the car that will be waiting under the arcades of the bank it is along this street that we will make our flight.)

The statue itself remains mysterious. The path on which it stands is almost perfectly bisected where two views join, but when the two photographs are laid side by side a space of one fifth of a centimetre on the scale of the photographs (nearly half a metre in reality) is missing, and the horse's head and the rider above, all but one hand extended in a rhetorical gesture, are in the gap. Another little imperfection in the photographer's art, but one that I find oddly re-assuring, since it is into just such a gap in reality (though rather wider, I hope, than a fifth of a centimetre) that I mean to slip in the moments after the crime. Having stepped out of my life to give the event, for that brief moment, the mind, the will, the trigger-finger it needs to come into existence. I shall step out again, as invisible and anonymous as that rider on the horse or our tourist/photographer, whose presence here we must take as given, since these views could hardly exist without him, but who is nowhere to be found in them and cannot be traced as their source.

So there it is, the Piazza Sant' Agostino at P. Of P. itself I know nothing; and of the square no more than I need to know. It is flagged, with big paving-stones, some of them stamped with the city's crest. It is closed on three sides with buildings, each of different centuries, and open to nature on the fourth. It has existed in this form since the 'nineties, and has been called the Piazza Sant' Agostino since the foundation of the church five centuries ago. Innumerable events have taken place here, some of them historical, some of them no more important than the appearance at the south door of the church of my two old women, who are commemorated in photographs one and two, the seven footballers with their invisible ball, and that crowd of young people whose presence here, and the shifting associations between them as they move from group to group, talking, exchanging gossip, making dates, will lead to other events – marriages, quarrels, bitter separations – too numerous to contemplate.

I have been in this square a hundred times in imagination. I shall enter it only once in fact, and may never know more of it than I do now, since the event itself, and the heart-slamming moments that lead up to it, will leave me no time for looking about to corroborate the thousand details I have stored in my memory. I shall be in the square for less than three minutes if all goes well. If it does not, the time, and the details, won't matter.

Meanwhile the event that will make this place notorious, that will take its name from the piazza and may prove to be the point in history towards which, through all the centuries, it was quietly moving, is still to occur, and only I can precipitate it. This knowledge gives my vision of the place an added dimension. It brings to the flat, black-and-white shots an excited glow as of a place that I have known already in a dream. And for me it will always be like this. Even when the brilliance of these separate visions has been dampened somewhat by real weather, and real sunlight being soaked up and reflected by stone. I have seen the square already in the light of its notoriety. After the event.

Someday in the future – let us say twenty years from now – I may return as a genuine tourist, though with a special interest; perhaps even in the company of a wife and child; stopping off out of whatever ordinary life I shall have slipped back into to revisit it. And in a sense I have already moved past the event to that nostalgic view that is inherent in the photographs, and perhaps in the very nature of photography itself. I am nostalgic for what has not yet occurred: for the darkness my first old lady is crossing towards, where the narrow street on the east side of the palace curves out of view; for the bean soup she will cook, and the headlines her husband will read aloud from the evening paper: ASSASSINATION AT P. This is the one indulgence I allow myself. It is purely aesthetic and therefore harmless.

But I wonder sometimes – to return to those gaps – how far I can trust my senses. I place my fingertips on the rusticated stone of the palace and try to feel the roughness. I try to judge whether the platform steps when I touch them are still sun-warmed or already cold. But imagination goes only so far into the world of touch, and though there is something to go on there is never enough. And how does the piazza smell? Of manure? Of fish? And is the sea audible at times under the hum of the traffic or when it pauses at the lights? I go back and back to the place and know from the triangle of shadow at its corner every uneven stone in the pavement. But I come as a man who is deaf, who cannot feel the warmth of the sun or the sudden coolness of shade, who has no sense of smell; a ghost, a tourist/photographer/assassin composed of nothing but mind.

It is to deal with at least one other of the senses that I imagine myself buying an icecream at the corner café.

Today the square tastes of chocolate. Tomorrow will be coffee and walnut, the day after pistaccio. A different flavour for each day of the week.

6

Do I need to name him, our great man of letters? He is a household word. Even those who have never read a line of the elaborate prose, whose authority is all in its fine distinctions, in its capacity to hold several opposing views in the same steady vision, may find one of his simple phrases on their lips in a moment of supreme emotion or will be aware at least that he is, at eighty, a rare national treasure and the last great figure of the age, a surviving witness to its many splendours and the long procession of its woes.

Essayist, philosopher, author of a dozen monuments to the art of narrative, he has created so much of our world that we scarcely know where history ends and his version of it begins. A whole stretch of the century lies exposed in his work: populations driven this way and that from farm to city – the poor, the hopeful, and those who already have no illusions – dark transports bearing them, across a countryside poised tremulously on the point of change, to factories, slave camps, pits of official slaughter, front line ditches at the edge of night. His vision is epic, and it is an epic strength that he brings to its depiction; yet no one has written more delicately, or with greater compassion and tact, of life's ordinary occasions, of first love, first tears, or the taste of that first mouthful of bread a boy pays for with his own earnings; of women seated alone with a suitcase in the waiting rooms of enormous stations, who have nowhere to go because they do not have the price of a ticket; of a child who eats apart in the playground to hide his secret shame – there is nothing in his lunch tin; of a youth so enamoured of his own purity that he cannot accept from the girl who comes to him her pure and common gift; of other, poorer youths brought face to face at last with their own future in the form of an examining committee or an agent of the law – Injustice in all its official regalia; of a workman, bestially drunk, who has been shamed once too often by his wife's forgiveness and beats her mercilessly in the public street. He has a special feeling for these dramas of the defeated. But for all his insistence on human folly and waste, and for all the darkness of his view, he never loses sight of the fact that day by day, even in the years of deepest horror, the life of things continues in the old patterns and according to the oldest and most ordinary rules. Spring arrives in the midst of battle with the same radiance of pear-blossom and hawthorn and little wild-flowers on banks in the wood. Birds sing above the slaughter. There is a harvest to be got in. A field of barley, sighing like the ocean, its long ears heavy with dew, has its own time-span and cannot wait another day to be brought in, whatever the facts of history. Grapes in September, olives in the clear cold days at the turn of the year. Wholeness and balance – that is the key-note. No other writer reminds us so often, or with such profound conviction, how much of our life is to be discovered, and enjoyed and made use of, in the narrow area between ecstasy and despair.

His conception of the task he has been set, and his strict dedication to its fulfilment, has created a body of work that fills a whole shelf above my desk, volume after volume of grace and light. It has also created the rather stiff and forbidding figure he presents in the photographs, the gaze direct, intense, but inward looking, its challenging frankness a kind of mask. He is, like his paragraphs, all of a piece; but a large piece that takes account of the contradictions and holds them in a precarious balance. 'This', he seems to say (he is not without humour) 'is my special trick. I do it well. It has taken me sixty years to achieve just this mixture of recklessness and ease.'

Pathetically fragile as a youth, and with a tendency to stoop, he has developed over the years a ramrod straightness, and suggests, with his clipped moustache and skullcap of cropped hair, the general of an imperial army, but one grander and nobler in its aspirations than any actual army of any nameable power. It is his struggles at the desk, and the keen self-discipline they necessitate, that has endowed his figure with hardness; as if the achievement of a perfect sentence imposed on the muscles the same rigours as a hundred press-ups or a half-hour's workout on the bars.

As a child he suffered from asthma and from all sorts of minor ailments. Today at eighty he has a constitution that would have astonished the youth of sixteen, and might even have embarrassed him with a robustness too common to be the vessel of extraordinary gifts.

Long-faced, tow-headed, he makes no impression at all in the family albums. He seems to be hiding from something. (Prompted by the author himself, we might guess at this distance that he was hiding from his fate.) It is the elder brother, the mother's favourite, son and heir to what there was of a family fortune, who catches the eye: a tall, clear-browed youth, utterly confident of his place in the world and of his own capacities, radiantly aglow with energy, and so impatient for the future that his glance already flashes beyond the restricting frame, his body seems already to have broken its formal pose, not by any movement of the casually settled limbs but in the animal spirit. He is a lion to the author's lamb.

Early pages of the *Memoir* make much of this contrast between the two brothers. They are filled with the freshness and splendour of the older boy's presence.

On a summer holiday on the Adriatic he is involved in a fist-fight with a young Austrian, and though badly beaten, his jacket torn, his cheek grazed and bruised, he walks away in the full retention of his spiritual ascendancy; the younger brother is much impressed by the light of solitary glory that plays about him as he wanders off through the *pineta,* and the incident becomes a model to which he returns over and over again, in more complex situations, of inner triumph in the face of defeat. The leader in all their childhood excursions, the giver of names to the objects of their common world, the recorder of its landmarks and mythologies, the older boy presides over these first years like a tutelary god.

His death, in the last weeks of the war, was not only the occasion of our author's earliest published work but the turning point, it might now appear, of his life. He has himself related how that first story leapt into existence and surprised him with the fact that he was a writer; and it is typical perhaps that the occasion should be, in retrospect, so full at the same time both of joy in the discovery of his own powers and an irremediable anguish.

He was preparing for his exams in the last days of summer, and had gone off to a favourite hiding-place to read, the top of an old oak tree beyond the orchard. It is famous now, he made it so, but was a special place even then in their secret geography of the region – a point of entry via its gnarled roots into the underworld, and upwards via its branches into the angels' realm.

He must have dozed off. Suddenly, starting awake, he became aware by a kind of sixth sense, before he could possibly have observed him, that his brother was there at the oak-tree foot staring quietly upward, afraid perhaps to startle him in that precarious cradle so high up in the boughs, and so quickened by the exertions of a fast sprint across the fields that the younger boy could hear the fetches of his breath. He must, he decided, have come home on an unexpected leave. He was simply standing, his face raised to the big tree's wealth of green, and breathing so deep in himself that the boy wondered if he had come to seek him after all and wasn't here on some business of his own, he was so completely absorbed in contemplation of the great rich canopy of leaves that poured its light upon him. He seemed too far off to be reached. But after hesitating a moment, the younger boy leaned down from his bough and called: 'I'm here. Come on up.'

The young man seemed caught off guard, as if he couldn't for the moment locate the source of the voice. Then he broke into one of his brilliant smiles, sprang into the boughs and began climbing.

But did not arrive. Passing out of sight for a moment in the thickness of the summer growth, he simply disappeared.

'I knew then,' the old man writes at a distance of nearly sixty years, 'that the few brief seconds in which I waited so breathlessly for him to reappear would become years, would become the whole of my lifetime. He was dead, I knew it quite clearly, in my blood, in the throbbing and quickening of my own pulse. Two days later the telegram arrived. But by then the little story, which had sprung fully developed into my head at first sight of him, had been written. He had given it to me complete, in that moment of staring up out of the darkness at the tree's foot. I have told nothing of this till now. It has been, for all these years, the obscure root out of which all my branches grew . . .'

It is a remarkable achievement, that first boyish effort; a vision of war in which his own imagination, and what he had heard at first hand from his brother, miraculously cohere to create out of children's games and boyish fantasies the whole horror of a generation's induction into the realities of war; a piece of local mythology transformed and expanded, a private vision shot through with the glare of history and made all the more significant by the author's youthful capacity to let everything he knows come flooding into the work, as if this might also be the last of it and he had no awareness yet of the sixty years that stretch so grandly before him, in which what he knows will find its full expression and for which something ought, after all, to be conserved. 'First works are like first love. Never again such prodigality – such thoughtless innocence.'

It was his brother's letters from the front that had done all this – not only opened his mind, in the deepest way, to the loss of youth and all its illusions among the abominations of war, but to those feelings of compassion for the ordinary man and his sufferings that have been so essential to his work. 'Through my brother's eyes', he tells us, 'I saw. That was the vision. And having seen could never forget.' The young god's death imposed upon him, all the more, his duty to remember and bear witness. 'Whenever I have been tempted as a writer to the merely brilliant and superficial, it is the shadow of his life, and the lives of so many in that generation, that falls across the page and recalls me to my solemn task. I began as a ghost writer. Perhaps I have remained one.'

Almost from the day of the brother's death (and his discovery of his own talent – since the two can hardly be separated) he ceased to stand at an oblique angle to the world. It is as if he had more air at last and could breathe deep. Suddenly precipitated into the centre of the family and loaded with the older boy's destiny he found the physical dimensions to fit it: he grew six centimetres in a single year, threw off his asthma, saw that first story, in which all his gifts appear in full flower, published and acclaimed, and arrived in a single bound at the threshold of a career.

In the light of all this, his claim to be no more than the older brother's ghost seems disingenuous, a little too good to be true. One senses rather the joy and confidence of being released into life at last, the transformation of old restrictions, old resentments even, into new forms of power. Like everything else about him, the moment of his brother's disappearance remains ambiguous; and one suspects that the elder boy, however attractive he may seem in the photographs, is little more than a literary device for the dramatization of his own leap into life. Genius is sly as well as candid. Was he perhaps the favourite child all along, that sickly heir-apparent – keeping out of the limelight, protecting himself from the need to be heroic, allowing the first born (as he comes close to suggesting on one occasion) to be the sacrificial victim that his generation demanded? Was he from the beginning the chosen one in the eyes of the gods?

Whatever the truth, he survived, and has come to see the shadowiness of his early life as part of a larger plan. The weakness nature gave him at the start was a way of conserving her own gift of strength, a first lesson that everything, even the gods' most abundant favours, must be recognized and grasped for.

Setting the photographs in chronological order, one observes the straightening and firming over the years of all his lines, but most of all the deepening at the bridge of his nose of two vertical creases like inverted commas – the imprint of a lifetime's devotion to irony. It is the development of a single theme. A slight nervousness, not to say slackness, in the too-pretty, rather girlish chin is there from beginning to end, but assumes over the years a new significance; so too does the tendency to dreaminess in the liquid eyes. These signs of weakness, of a secret complicity with the forces of disintegration, of sensuality, of illness even, are never quite subdued to the austerity of the whole; they remain to complicate the picture, and as the face discovers its sterner characteristics, so the chin becomes finer, more nervously attuned to what tempts to indulgence, the eyes grow deeper, more dreamy. It is as if eyes and chin belonged to a different style of life from the strict mouth and the inverted commas above the nose; brought him news of the underworld; belonged to the author of what he likes to call his anti-Works, those dark, unwritten masterpieces that are in an opposing spirit to his own but are their shadowy complement. It is part, all this, of that delicate balance between moral strictness and a disarming openness to the destructiveness of things that is his signature and constitutes his 'special trick'.

What better example than the essay on Julian the Apostate, so bold, so ardent, so extravagantly wilful, in which the prose itself, phrase by phrase, responds to the two sides of his nature, the natural bohemian and pagan sensualist and that grim apostle of rule and order, that worshipper of the stern god? Impossible in these pages to pin the author down, as his nature turns now this way now that, and his thought moves, in its monumental but oddly quick-footed and quick-witted way, among church ceremonies, theological disputes, banquets, assignations, court intrigues – endlessly shifting between fastidious disapproval and an almost breathless realization of the enticements of the flesh. (The commentators fly amusingly in both directions, like messengers scattering from a battlefield to announce simultaneously, and by their own lights accurately, both triumph and defeat.)

It has always been the same. Invited in the 'thirties, when imperial glory was the very stuff of our daily lives, to contribute to the birthday honours of the regime's favourite historian, he first declined, then hesitated, then ruefully accepted, then produced nothing at the right time, then, at the wrong time, not the middle-length essay he had been asked for but a whole brilliant book, a flight of scholarly fancy on the subject of Roman drains that was immediately taken up by the opposition and read, in all its twistings and turnings through the intestinal underworld of the imperial ideal, the darkness under crowded theatres and stadia and forums, as a deliberate attack on the notion of empire itself.

A savage battle raged, from which he remained grandly aloof, expressing nothing but surprise at the way his little researches had been taken: 'Scatology? Do they really think so? Subversive? My humble drains?'

Friends pointed out the danger he was in and urged him to flee. He shrugged and prevaricated; but before the authorities could come to their ponderous decision, took his wife and the three much-photographed children and went, carrying with him all his household effects: library, stamp collection, Persian rugs, cabinet of antique coins and bronzes; but defiantly, under the very nose of the police.

There followed six years of voluntary exile, first in Switzerland, then in Argentina. They proved of course to be the most productive years of all. When he returned he was indisputably The Master, but with his wife dead and the majority of his friends and contemporaries dispersed or done away with – victims of the convulsions of those years – it was a lonely triumph. Cut off from the new generation, a survivor it might seem from the far side of history, he withdrew, and has over the years become more and more inaccessible, more remote in his solitary grandeur; and this too has added to the lofty image he presents and the power of his presence among us as a sacred monster.

There are photographs as well as volumes of richly worked prose to illustrate this. I lay them out on the desk and use a magnifying glass to bring them close.

Item: from his years of research on the imperial drains a casually perfect image from the ruins at Sabratha. The great man, all clipped and smooth in a light grey suit, with a cane over his shoulder and his thin moustache prematurely whitened by the North African sun, leans diagonally across the frame, in parody one might think of a matinee idol from the cinema or a music-hall performer. On his thin lips there is just the flicker of a smile. As at some subterranean jest. 1933.

Item: from the following year something less poised and formal. He appears as *pater familias* under a striped beach umbrella, with his wife, the three children and the various paraphenalia of their summer play – beach buckets and spades, a ball and an inflatable shark or dolphin, it is difficult to tell which, that the little group has laughingly included as the family pet.

These were happy years. They went out a good deal, the famous couple, and were photographed in many fashionable places. His extraordinary energy involved him in literary activities outside his fiction – criticism, controversy. They were the centre of a brilliant group. They gave parties, had other famous people to stay for the weekend, kept three houses, one in the mountains and another on the coast as well as an establishment in Rome that had always, outside the sacred hours of his labour, an open door for unexpected guests. Fate, and history, had not yet intervened to make a recluse of him.

Item: two snapshots from the Swiss period.

In one the writer is caught (if that is the right word) in his garden. He is again suited in grey, with a checkered bow-tie, and is on this occasion holding in his left hand a straw boater that seems almost transparent in the late afternoon light, a discarded halo. He is leaning forward to examine a rose. To examine it, I mean, in the inquisitorial sense; asking it to account for itself, to say precisely what it means or understands by its own being. He looks faintly amused by the rose's discomfort at being faced, and so publicly, with a *personage*; and one whose mere presence in the garden calls everything else into question. 'See what a terror I can be,' he seems to be saying. 'even when I am off duty, even when I am in nature. Such are the rigours of the moral life. Such it is to have greatness thrust upon one. Isn't it a tremendous joke? But tell me this, little rose, am I really the great man himself or just a child dressed up in the great man's clothes?'

In the second of these snapshots he does not appear, but one guesses from the amateurishness of the pose – the family strung out in a single line with three jagged peaks behind them – that the camera was in his hand, and that the distorted shadow that falls across it is his.

The wife Elena is looking away in brilliant profile. The children, two girls and a boy – one girl a leggy twelve year-old, the other just out of the plump infant stage, the boy sitting cross-legged and engagingly alert in knickerbockers and cap – are staring straight into the sun, and are touched for the contemporary viewer by what he knows is already moving towards them out of the decades to come.

The boy will be finished at twenty-two in a shooting

accident. For all his sturdiness he has been bequeathed, and in large measure, the fineness of the famous chin, that pointer to a world of decadence that our great man keeps at a distance with stern discipline, allowing it just enough scope to give fantasy, drama and a sense of risks grandly taken, to his prose. The boy, not knowing the rules of that perilous game, and having no 'special trick' of his own, will take the fiction for fact; he will catch from the swamp element in his father's imagination a chronic fever.

The youngest child will enter an asylum on the far side of one of those sparkling alps, not a hundred kilometres as the crow flies, as the black crow flies, from where she is now standing.

Only the elder daughter will find the strength to survive. But it is the strength of a nature unqualified by any touch of lightness. She will thicken into the sour fifty-year-old, her father's keeper, who will be at his side, guiding him towards me with a strong hand, when we come to the event.

The truth is that his special trick depends upon his playing, quite deliberately, with forces that he is by nature immune to and others are not. He flirts with destructive passions – madness, perversion, the flight into illness – to test his own capacity to resist, to call up the correlative and bracing forces that add tension to his work. But the poisonous vapours released do not immediately disperse. They hang about him; they are transferred from his imagination to the imagination of others and assume real forms there that they are powerless to resist. Commentators sometimes speak of him as a tragic figure, as a man to whom the gods have granted every favour but one: he has suffered the loss, one after another, of all those who were dearest to him. I wonder. Like all great men he is at heart an egoist, and dangerous. His wife in the Swiss photograph seems already used up. Her staring away out of the frame is like a first step to freedom; she has set her face against something – Argentina? (She will die on the voyage out and be consigned to the waters off Grand Canary.) The thin-legged girl seems already to have been offered up in her mother's place.

There are times when simply to expose oneself to the hypnotic beauties of his style, to enter the labrynthine sentences with their tortuous flashings and flarings, is to run the risk of a special sort of corruption, the corruption of the moral. I have come to distrust his high-toned achievements at the very moment when I am most deeply moved by them. I have begun to develop a nose, among all that beautiful architecture, all those noble vistas, those pediments and finials, for the smell of drains – a faculty he might recognize and approve and for which he might bestow upon me, from his great height, a little half-smile of sympathetic approval, the pleasure of a Master at the glimmerings of a slow pupil who improves.

But I should confess that if, through long sessions of study, I have begun to understand him a little, to observe, that is, the dangers that are inherent in the very nature of his 'trick', he has also, and so long ago that it quite scares me, both understood and accounted for me.

Imagine the quickening of my pulse, the cold gathering of sweat on my brow, when I first encountered that novella of his, completed in Argentina in 1939, nearly a decade before I was born, in which he describes the assassin of Professor Celario, the ambassador at Santo Domingo. It is as if he had, in some uncanny way, by one of those intuitions that have about them a touch of the demonic and bring a whiff of black magic, of smouldering flesh, to even the freshest of his pages, taken a quick look down the tunnel of his life and seen me, in the merest flash of a second, standing before him with the revolver in my hand. But not me exactly. Rather a foreshadowing of me in the shape of a young man waiting at a tramstop in Zurich, wearing the garments, as he describes it, of an interesting event, and behind the Zurich youth another, glimpsed the previous summer on the Ramblas at Barcelona, in whom he had sensed just that mixture of subdued violence, idealism, recklessness and nostalgia for the impossibly heroic that was floating about in those middle years of the decade and which he would embody in the seminary student Francesco.

The vision can have given him no more than a fleeting glimpse, and I am not Francesco; but he had seen me just the same. Reading his dark analysis, his infernal speculations about the origins of violence in our age, I felt myself first hot, then cold, as if a hand had been laid upon me in the silence and I might be recognized by any passer-by in the street. I felt anger as well. As if all the things I have so painfully discovered and fought for in my life were, after all, quite common and ordinary – predicted, described, made public a decade before my birth.

Is this an example of how he works, this capacity to grasp a whole text by turning up the merest corner of it, this entering so deeply into the form of things that the very process of their being is made available to him through a single detail, and so completely that his energy need only fill their form in space a moment to recreate their whole life and momentum? I imagine the wry tightening of his lips as he perceives that he has already comprehended me and that I can therefore be dismissed. His superiority is insufferable. I feel as if he had publicly humiliated me, even if no one knows it but myself. Is this mere brooding? He has exposed me as a worm; not because his picture of the young assassin is unsympathetic – on the contrary, as so often in his writing he has discovered as many aspects of the anarchist killer in himself as the noble ambassador – but because what he has so amply set down is, he believes, the whole of what I am and only the smallest particle of himself, because in comprehending me he has also written me off.

A good many of my hours here are devoted to a secret turning of the tables on him. I examine the stiff twenty-year-old, staring boldly past the camera with his high white collar and cap, circa 1919, and the borrowed assurance of his dead brother; or the proprietorial young genius, already the darling of the connoisseurs, upright behind the chair where his new bride sits smiling, one hand on his watch-chain, the other resting, very lightly, on her shoulder; or the figure caught 'among contemporaries' on the quayside at Rhodes, disguised now in beard and panama, turning a glass in his hand; and I say to myself, 'I know where you are heading, sir, and you do not. We may add all these facts and images to one another to make a perfect record of your life, and throw in the novels, the essays, the newspaper articles, the letters, your ambassadorial regalia, your medals, your honourary degrees (including the one from Oxford), and all the unhappy history of your family, and what will be missing is a tiny fact that I have in my head and which does not exist as yet in yours. It casts a different light on all this. It subtly changes the portrait of the twenty-year-old genius because it establishes at last what he was peering at so intently across the years and could not make out: the muzzle of a revolver. It is what accounts for those two little creases in the brow that will deepen with the years. It is the third beside you (proprietorial) and your young wife (with her eye already on the sea off Grand Canary) in the wedding photograph. Its shadow falls across the brilliant conversation, changing the weather of that morning at Rhodes and transmuting even the colours of the half-finished drinks. The place and manner of your death – that I have in *my* possession. It doesn't make things even between us, nothing could. But it helps.

Still, I regret that when we do meet at last it will be too late to ask the questions I would like to put to him and which I have come to feel only he can answer. Our conversations remain imaginary; and my imagination is weak. I go back again and again to the hints he has let drop of what he might have to say to me: a few exchanges of the ambassador and his assassin, that are charged with significance and irony but remain inexplicit, since neither knows the part he is to play in the other's life; something to be read between the lines of the 'Letter to a Son'; something again in a note on 'The Present Generation' where he takes as his text, with a playfulness that is not without malice, a passage from Chateaubriand: 'We must speak of a state of soul which, it seems to me, has still to be described: it is that which precedes the development of great passions, when all the young, active, self-willed, yet restricted faculties are exercised only upon themselves, with neither goal nor aim. The more a race advances towards civilization, the more is augmented this condition of the vagueness of the passions. Finally there occurs a sad situation: the great number of examples which one has before one's eyes, the multitude of books which deal with man and his feelings, make the individual clever without having experienced life. He becomes undeceived without having been deceived. Some desires remain, but there are no more illusions. With a full heart one inhabits an empty world, and without having made use of anything, we are dissatisfied with all there is.' Does he realize how the dismissiveness of that may have worked to make some of us – one of us at least – break out of empty dreaming into the world of events?

Of all his various characters, and I am speaking now not only of his writing but of his life as well, it is the son

I feel closest to, dead at twenty-two in a shooting accident which is also, by one of those exchanges of fact and fiction that occur so often in the great man's vicinity, prefigured with uncanny accuracy of detail in one of the *Tales*. But there is nothing more to be discovered in that quarter. The boy makes his brief appearance in family photographs and in clippings here and there from the magazines. He is said to be writing a novel, but it never appears. He does publish poems, but they are not distinguished. He organizes a safari to East Africa and is photographed with lions; he joins a yachting party to the Greek Islands. Then, out of the blue, the accident, and a year later, on the boy's birthday, the 'Letter'.

It is a work that angers me. I resent it, as the son might also have done had he lived to receive it. There is no doubting the old man's grief; he recalls the early years of his own career when the boy was born, adding one or two of those charming touches that are his alone, in which we glimpse something of the young father's pride and affection and something too of the boy's early grace and promise. But there are no letters from the son, no youthful outpouring of reproach or self-justification to which the great letter might be a reply. What the occasion produces is yet another display of stoic fortitude, another act of dedication to the task, and once again – a response we might feel to the demands of the writing itself for 'difficulty' – the insistence on 'taking things hard', on putting himself to the test, on going deep into his nature to track down, at the centre of each labrynthine paragraph, the secret that would hide there and must be dragged into the light and challenged, and disposed of in a cleansing gush of blood. The drama is impressive, so is the passion for truth. But somehow one is embarrassed by the surge of renewed energy that comes to him with this new stroke of fate, the opportunity it offers to show once again his powers of mastery. *The work, the Work.* Everything in the end becomes simply another proof of his extraordinary genius, his capacity to turn life's bitter hardships into the stuff of art.

I say 'simply'; but of course nothing about him is simple. Neither are the reactions he inspires. For the grandeur of the task he has set himself and his patient dedication to its completion I am all admiration. He too is a skier on Everest, and if we find within us the notion of such an ideal, it has been learned from him. (An irony he might savour, this: that he should provide, from the moral point of view, a model for his own killer.) Can genius be separated from egotism? His ego is monstrous; yet it is in the protean transformation and masquerades of this ego, its capacity to slip in and out of other forms, other lives, that he discovers that feeling for the oneness of things that both justifies his vision of himself as a phenomenon of nature and convinces us of its truth. I think of him carrying his precious gift, his ego, before him, like a tribal vessel in which all our destinies are to be read, and have an almost impersonal curiosity about the moment when it will fall from his grasp. It is that sound, its shattering on the stones of the Piazza Sant'

Agostino at P., rather than the shot, his small cry, the daughter's shrill one – it is the thought of that sound, scattering the pigeons across the cathedral façade, filling the square with footsteps, that moves me, and fills me at times with a kind of terror at the enormity of what I am to do.

Tuning my ears carefully as I read – his letters, his stories – I can just hear, faintly between the lines, the first pre-echo of that sound as it lifts and rolls towards me.

7

In cutting myself off from the past and relinquishing every object that might identify me I have made one exception; it is a small one, a variegated pebble I found as a child on the beach at M. and have kept ever since as a talisman. Antaeus retained his strength so long as he could touch the earth, and I suppose we are meant to understand by this fable that there is between us and nature a channel through which energy endlessly flows, and feeds us and keeps us whole. For me, if the analogy doesn't seem pretentious, the earth has contracted to this pebble, once rough-edged, but worn now to a smoothness by years of being turned between thumb and forefinger, as it might, if I had left it out there, have been worn to the same shape by the sea. (I have intervened and changed nothing!)

It is grey, it looks undistinguished. But in certain lights, and when polished by the slight moisture of the fingertips, it reveals hidden colours; muted, but to the practised eye, of a quite brilliant range, like a winter sunset. As a child I used to lie with it so close to my nose that all proportion was lost and I could imagine myself spread out on a clifftop in Sumatra or Peru, watching the tropic sun go down in a vivid light-show on the horizon; or sometimes, in a submarine mood, found myself peering through a thin pane into the mid-ocean depths. Its light could even be perceived with the fingertips, as when, for example, during an examination or in some moment of confrontation in the playground, I turned the pebble in my pocket and felt the occasion instantly transform itself, saw it shot through with new colours, new possibilities, felt myself come to earth as it were, ever so lightly, as if I too had been transformed in proportion with it, on the pebble's smooth translucent surface. Held to the ear like a closed shell I could hear waves in it; not of the sea but from space, a steady beating. Held on the palm of my hand I saw reflected in it the far side of the universe, invisible to us, from which it might have fallen as a fragment of some scattered meteor, still in touch (and I through it) with a million other particles elsewhere, all of them responsive still to the tide of energy from 'out there'.

Schoolboy fancies, all. But they have persisted. Not because I believe them, or have been unable to give up a childish habit of thought, but because they evoke in me real responses that have nothing to do with the fantastic and which still nourish and sustain the spirit.

So: this fragment of my past, this pebble. Always there, a tiny added weight, in my left-hand pocket among the change. I think of it as a source of strength, but it might, I suppose, be my last weakness. A comforter. As a small child I used to let it sleep in my mouth like an all-day sucker, and liked the notion of its being worn smooth there by the words I uttered round it; till my father objected to the impediment in my speech. Now somehow that notion appeals to me again: a stone worn smooth by speech, every syllable, true or false, making its small change in the shape of the thing. Of course I am too old for such nonsense, but I think perhaps, if taken in and questioned, it might comfort me to have the old stone in the corner of my jaw, to taste its no-taste as of space, and to recognize the power of distortion its presence would create and the odd light it might throw on my 'story' – a lurid glow.

I finger it as I write. Does it add its lurid glow even to this?

8

My father comes from a family with land holdings in the south, in Calabria and Sicily. He cut all ties with that feudal world more than thirty years ago, when he was still a student, invested what money he had in a farm, and has lived ever since the life of a gentleman peasant, managing all the farmwork himself and spending his spare time reading, playing the flute, indulging a taste for obscure scientific speculations and mounting one of the country's largest collection of beetles. He is an old-fashioned radical, and believes, I think, that our great mistake was to have left the eighteenth century. He has settled there very happily himself, with just the sort of uncomfortable rigour that would, he affirms, be the salvation of us all. Though fiercely anti-clerical he is not at all irreligious. To watch him surveying, in the early light of a summer morning, a field of wheat that is ready to be harvested, all afire in the dewy moments after sunrise, is to see a man solemnly absorbed in the oldest form of worship. With all this he has a high regard for machinery and is a subscriber to the best journals of contemporary science. He is, I think, almost entirely admirable and a little foolish. In which he once again remains faithful to his chosen century.

For example, nothing that lives, not even a viper, may be killed on his land. When the local electrical authority claimed the right to run power-lines through a section of his woods, he first fought them in the courts, and then, when he had been defeated at last, made them paint the poles. They stand out all the more clearly now, a liverish green, against the changing colour of the hills, and his point is established, but against the grain, not with it. Having first denied the twentieth century, and being forced at last to see it come marching across his property, he has the satisfaction at least of having exposed its vulgarity. His real master is Quantz, whose flute sonatas and studies fill his evening hours; in despite he would want to claim of their original performer, whom he thinks of as a false hero of the age and whose presence, perhaps, his devotion to the flute is intended to exorcise; he is re-writing history. I hope I describe him with all the ironical affection I feel for this old man who is my father, and make it clear that there is nothing in what I have chosen to do that is in any way meant to defy or shock him. It is not my father I have set out to kill. That sort of psychological short-hand is just what he most despises in our century, and in that way I am his true son.

I write to him regularly and look forward to his long, carefully composed replies, with their news of confirmations in the world of astronomy or astrophysics of his own intuitions. One might believe that giant telescopes in the Arizona desert or in Siberia are nightly tilted at the heavens on his behalf, to prove a contention that has long made him seem harmlessly crazy to his friends, and that quasars, and all sorts of other phenomena, spring into existence only so that he can say, 'There, I told you so! Your father isn't such an old fool after all', or to win an argument taken up twenty years ago with one of his eighteenth-century antagonists, or with my mother, who was religious in the conventional sense and regarded all those scientific interests of his that couldn't be pinned to a board and named, and numbered, as little better than witchcraft. A good deal of his talk to me, I have often suspected, is really directed at my mother, whom I barely knew. I do not resent this either. It makes me feel closer to both of them. What I know best of my mother is what he recognizes in me that he can speak to.

It disturbs me that in this period of isolation I am forbidden to write to him. Several weeks ago I manufactured half a dozen postcards, affectionate jottings that are to be posted to him from London at intervals of a week or so till I am released. I have a clear image of him tramping down to the postbox to collect these cards, carrying them up to the house, finding his spectacles and deciphering the brief, false messages. What worries me especially, I think, is the tampering with time. Choosing to write to him from a point three weeks ahead, a postcard from the future, I might equally have postdated the card February 1998, or backdated it to the day Leibnitz died. The ambiguities of shape and direction that are inherent in our idea of time he will argue about by the hour; but he would be affronted, I think, to find me playing ducks and drakes with it in this trivial and easy way. Quite apart from what he might feel about the deception as it touches him, I am treading here on holy ground and being as blasphemous as if I had despatched a series of directives to him in the name of the Holy Ghost.

I saw him last five months ago. He likes me, when I can, to come and spend a few days in the only place I have ever thought of as home; to restore my links with the house itself, but also, since it is in the familiar objects and order of the house that he has settled our relationship, things that are clear and tangible, with himself as well. The familiar warmth of the stone kitchen on early winter mornings, as we sit together at the wooden table drinking coffee from chipped bowls while half a dozen dogs stretch on the flags and newborn puppies moil about in a basket beside the range, or the deep shadows the farmhouse beams make in the light thrown upward by lamps – these are not simply qualities of the place but stages in the day's progress, that have, over long years, become the visible conditions of our common life, all the more deeply felt because they seem independent of us and have only to be stepped back into to be renewed. A house may establish a state of feeling as well as a design for living.

He is a believer in deep continuities, my father, in the shaping influence of scenes and objects on the inner life; these, and the seasonal routines of the farm. To draw me back into them occasionally, into the rituals of my earliest childhood, is he feels to re-enforce for me the clear line of my movement through space and time, even if it has been a movement away.

I am not so sure. But the place itself, and the slow pace of our lives there, in which even our walking is determined by the slope of a field or the roughness of a path on which rain has exposed all the original rocks, the dependence of our diet on the capacity of the land itself to produce in its various seasons this crop, that vegetable – broadbeans, runnerbeans, artichokes, tomatoes, zucchini – imposes its own pattern, and releases us, since it is the pattern of an earlier existence, from what is merely 'modern'. Or seems to. Moving together in it to repair a roughstone wall, or sweating to clear some patch of the orchard that has gone too quickly to blackberry scrub, going through the motions of one of the immemorial tasks of this countryside, as on ladders set at different angles we work fast at the stripping of an olive, the same fruit on the same branch, discovering again, in the rhythms of the work, a silent community – all this is restorative of the old relationship between us, and in my case at least (for he does not change) of an earlier self that I fall back into as soon as my body adapts to the routine of swift, mindless work. The mind lapses, afloat in a slow dream of doing just this and nothing else through all eternity, of working high up in the light of ancient branches, tumbling the fruit into a basket, or when the hand misses, letting it fall into a net. That earlier self is not lost in me, though I reject it. It is for his sake, but perhaps also for my own, that I come back two or three times a year and let it emerge.

Last November, when I was preparing myself for my life here and had in spirit already entered it, I went to visit him for what I knew might be the last time. My lack of absolute presence cannot have escaped him, though he would never have mentioned it.

It was, I know, his favourite time of year, as it is also mine. The countryside is at its barest, showing clearly again its original lines, the fruit trees already stripped, and the woods, in the hollows between fields or on the mountains behind, all the darker and greener for having the scene to themselves at last. The fields, newly ploughed, show all the earth colours, from silver-grey and blond through brown of every shade to the richest loamy black, looking oddly, where plough-lines take shadow in the evening light, as if lengths of woven fabric had been spread to air, knitwear or tweed, and above them the high rinsed skies, with tons of water swirlingly suspended above the blue.

Everything is at a point of rest. The land is waiting to be sown and for the first rain. Stove-lengths of holm-oak, mulberry, acacia have been brought in and stacked in rectangles at the edge of a path. The olive picking is done. There are long stretches of time to be filled with flute-playing in the early afternoon and with small tasks like the mending of tools, the preparing of canes for next year's staking. It is a time of talk; of standing at boundary fences and listening regretfully to the *pock pock* of rifles as hunters drop pheasants on the far side of a hill or the confused medley of sound, horses, dogs, the shouts of men and the reverberation of big double-barrelled shot-guns, at a boar hunt.

Something of the tension between these two aspects of the scene, the land's intense stillness and suspension and the eruption of the sounds of hunting, of men gratuitously imposing their will on things, is what attracts me to this time of year: argument and counter argument, dreamlike stasis and abrupt, violent activity. It would not be the same without its small, unnecessary deaths.

It is a tension that I associate with adolescence, when I first began to think for myself and found, not without pain, that some of what my father most deeply believed and had taught me I could no longer accept. I bought a shotgun, which I kept at a neighbour's house, and I too, when the season came, stalked the wet fields and took my toll of the birds. It was a first disloyalty. My father never found out; or if he did he kept me from my own shame and gave no sign of it. Something of the static quality of the autumn landscape, that sense I had then of being held back from action but criminally freed, still haunts me. It is the landscape of my youth. Though in fact it is my father, these days, who plays the adolescent – the shy, secretive one, full of dreamy yearnings and fulfilments that he cannot reveal.

For the past three years he has had a woman, a village girl not much older than myself, who cooks, cleans the house, looks after a herb garden and chicken-run beyond the kitchen, makes jam, fills the window sills with pots of red and pink geranium and is altogether good-humoured, thoughtful, efficient and clearly fond of him. The house is filled with her companionable warmth, and the occasional flash beyond a door of her pretty headscarfs, and it isn't only the glow of polish and elbow grease that she imposes on all its scattered bits and pieces. I hear her singing sometimes, but the moment she catches my footfall she stops, as if even that might be a presumption I would resent. She serves us in the dining-room at lunch and dinner, quietly fetching and carrying and then eating alone afterwards in the kitchen; but when I am not here they must eat together, either by the kitchen fire or on the terrace, and when I caught them once in the tail-end of an argument, it was, I knew, over her refusal to drop this pretence and share the table with us. But that would have been a declaration that might have involved every piece of furniture in the room.

It was a declaration he wanted to make and which I would have welcomed, but some delicacy of feeling, either on my behalf or the woman's, prevented him. It would have made things easier between us and would have allowed me to move about the house without fear of stumbling on something awkward. As it was I had to pretend that I didn't notice the flow of energy between them whenever she entered a room or when she moved about the table as we ate, the attraction of his attention away from whatever we were discussing, his quickened, almost boyish excitement. More than anything else it made me feel old; as if we had switched generations. In my self-conscious adolescence it would never have entered my head to sleep with one of the girls who came to cook or clean for us; though he must, I suppose, have expected it and kept his eye open for a betraying gesture; as I tried now to keep mine closed.

I had wanted before I left to say something to him or at least to give him a hint that I understood and approved. Especially on the last night, when after our silent meal we had to go out and search the thicket for a strayed sheep.

It was a still cold night full of stars. Thin mist lay in the wooded pockets, but the fields above were silver in the moonlight and as we strolled back we heard the woman's voice from the house; it must have been magnified by the stillness of the night. She was washing dishes at the sink and singing. He stopped to catch the sound, just as we passed the point where it became audible, and I felt him, after that, being drawn on its long, sure thread. A full-throated singing in the old style – a tune that might have gone back centuries, solemn but not sad, and for him an essential quality of the night itself, so that when we paused at the gate to light our cigarettes and he said, not at all embarrassed, 'It's so beautiful; I feel sometimes that I might live for ever,' he was speaking equally of both, the strong hold of the woman's voice and the moonlit land under its ceiling of winter cloud.

'Do you think at all of getting married?' he asked me suddenly.

I saw that what he was really telling me was that he would like a grandchild, that that sort of continuity was also in his mind. The woman's voice drew him to the house, but for my sake, and for this, he would delay his going.

'Perhaps,' I said. 'Yes, certainly. In time.'

'Good. It's a fine thing, marriage. I wouldn't want you to miss it.'

He rested his hand very lightly on my arm, then moved off. 'When you were away in America' he said, 'I thought you might never come back.'

I shook my head in the dark, and it was then that I might have spoken, warned him in some way that I had work to do that might take me further from him than I had ever been before, though that too would make no break between us. But it was too late. We were already in the clear light that leapt from the house. The girl had seen us and stopped singing. We were at the boundaries of that early morning silence in which we would breakfast together, finding words only for the yelping and nuzzling dogs, and part on the local platform with only the briefest and most formal embrace, an assurance that everything between us was as it had been and would be always, but with nothing said on either side of what was closest to our hearts.

9

I know every detail of his daily routine. He is, after all, a worker like ourselves, tied, as he has been for more than fifty years, and wherever he might find himself, to a regimen that has, in all that time, barely varied. He is both Master and slave.

Wakes at a quarter past seven to the thin piping of swallows glimpsed in the oblong of the half-open window, their reflection cutting so vividly across its watery light that they seem at moments, by some special trick of their own, to have slipped through into another dimension, since they are nowhere in the room.

Little bodies made of water and dust, the realest thing about them their cries, they are wheeling and dipping in the great well of air below the sill, following the flight of insects, swerving so close to the wall in their frenzied hunger that the shutter, and sometimes even the window-glass, is splashed with their droppings – a nuisance to the girl who has to come and scrape it off, but to him, as he tells us in the *Memoir*, a kind of comic blessing. Especially when a small pile lands splat on his desk; or even – O sacrilege! – on one of his sacred pages, and dries to a crust, and so finds its way into an American library.

The room at S., seven kilometres from P., is a big front room in the second story with French windows to a balcony. There is a view, to judge from the pictures, across low hills, a patchwork of olive groves and vineyards, and on clear days a flash of the sea.

It is the country of his childhood and the house is the one he was born in. He has come, as he says, full circle: one life, a single gesture, the breath and the work.

The room and its contents he has already described in the first chapter of the *Memoir.* I paraphrase.

Walls white – though they were, in his mother's day, pale blue, and there are tiny patches of blue still visible (he has tracked them down, every one, these remnants of the blue skies of his youth) in odd places round the skirting boards and high up in corners under the beams. 'Thankful I am, on occasion,' he tells us, 'for the slapdash workmen of this region, who have left me these scraps of earlier days, the blue of my childhood and youth, to launch back into on invisible parachutes. *Ecco!* We are back in the first days of the century, in mama's room, taking a sip of her early morning chocolate . . .'

The walls, now, white, and the curtains also white; an austerity broken only by two eighteenth-century landscapes in rococo frames, and on the sofa-table a fine pre-Columbian terracotta of the earth mother, half human, half animal, squatting in the act of birth.

A bed of the high old-fashioned sort, with brass rails

and finials and a cover in hand-worked crochet. To the right a walnut commode that once housed a chamber-pot, now his night table, and on the marble top an oil-lamp converted to electricity, with a beautifully moulded hood in mother-of-pearl glass. When it is lighted, softly aglow above the fields, it is as if a jellyfish, one of the great medusas, had wandered in from the sea and were pulsing and pulsing, making its way through the depths towards dawn. Besides the lamp, his moderate requirements for the night: pills, a pad and pencil, a tumbler of water covered with a lace cloth.

There are two comfortable chairs in the room, one of them set permanently with its back to the window; it is where he reads in the afternoon. A cabinet for papers, a sofa-table, the big desk – nothing more. Rugs in the winter, the worn stone floor in summer. To the left his bathroom and dressing room, to the right the corridor.

Six days a week he lives and works here, going down only to stroll for an hour before tea on the lawn above the garden and to dinner at eight-thirty. No more visits to the theatre, no public engagements, no trips.

Everything timed precisely.

At seven-fifteen the daughter appears with coffee and an English water biscuit. She kisses his brow, sets down the wooden tray with its worn picture from the Villa of Mysteries at Pompeii, puts his slippers in place on the rug, goes into the room next-door to run his bath-water and lay out his clothes. At seven-thirty he bathes and dresses. At eight-thirty – at the very moment when I am settling at my own desk in the office, to go through my photographs and clippings – he lays out papers, unscrews his pen and begins. He likes to work these days in the room where he sleeps, with the bed in which he takes his night-journeys neatly made behind him, a counterweight to the heavy desk, and the script that rises to fill the blank pages continuous now with his dreams. The swallows are still screaming in circles below. The sound of a tractor can be heard from a nearby field, and from the yard the voices of women. A ground-bass: reality. The words appear.

He writes steadily till just before twelve, when the dog Manfred, a german shepherd, is let in to be wrestled with a little and to lick his hands.

The dog, of course, is famous – either this dog or one of its forebears. A whole essay has been devoted to him, another proof that for the writer material is always to hand, and more of it than he can ever deal with; all there in the room, or in his head. The dog, the domesticated wolf, is the starting point for a disquisition on the long relationship between man and the animal kingdom of which man is himself a part, on the creative energy, the moral energy even, that belongs to our animal nature, its essential innocence, and on our need to make contact with it again, to find our way back into the garden and lie down, in all our dangerous knowledge and power, with the beasts.

The dog is led out again when his daughter appears with his lunch, and she also takes with her whatever he has spent the morning composing. Further paragraphs of an article, or passages to be worked into the *Memoir*, which will be given its final shape only when he has come to the end of these desultory excursions from which, with all the joy of a child stumbling down from the attic, he brings back brilliant fragments of his life that have not yet found expression in some other form, bits of surviving blue, as he puts it, that the careless workman overlooked and which have the virtue now of being living relics from another age. Or there will be two or three pages of a new novel, parts of which appear regularly in the magazines.

This 'Work in Progress' has a special poignancy. It is, strangely enough, the most youthful thing he has ever done – some commentators might say the only youthful thing he has done. Lighter in touch, more daring than anything he would have attempted in his great days or even ten years ago, it is a kind of scherzo in which his deepest themes reappear in travesty, as if, behind all their grandeur, their imperious graspings after the ideal, their noble solemnities, we were invited to see a group of children dressed up in their parents' clothes, the attic finery of a vanished era. *Child's play,* he calls it; something he had to go back to the house of his childhood and his own beginnings to discover, little lively skeletons who have got out of the closet and are making a jolly row (it is his own expression) on the stairs.

Below, in a room at the back of the house, his morning pages will be typed by a young woman, a student, who comes in for two hours each afternoon and is paid by the page.

She is closely supervised by the daughter, who gave up this task only two years ago and finds a good deal to complain about in the cleanness of the girl's copies; though their aesthetic quality is in fact irrelevant, since the old man will cover them with a dense network of revisions in his small, rather crooked hand. It is on these typed pages, he tells us, that the real work is done. 'Second thoughts, always second thoughts, qualifications, digressions, inspired elaborations. The ground work, yes; that comes straight up from the dark like a strong stem, single and full of sap. The second thoughts, unfolding brilliantly out of the first, are the full tree's lovely greenness.'

When he has finished lunch, rested for an hour and read for another hour with his back to the light from the window, the typed pages are brought up to him, together with a coffee, and he will sit at his desk and let his second thoughts into the room. Then at four-thirty he takes his stick, calls for the dog and goes down to take a walk. The day's work is finished and ready to be typed up.

It is all very methodical. Working thus over the years, keeping steadily to the routine, one creates books enough to fill whole shelves in a library and to keep scores of students at work on bibliographies, variant texts, critical studies of patterns and variations; not to speak of the letters, whole crates of them. He still writes four or five each day, in the late afternoon between five-thirty and seven, keeping carbons of the originals that his daughter will file, according to date and recipient, in the cabinet downstairs.

His day now is almost over. Dinner at eight-thirty; alone with the daughter (who has the household's little happenings to relate – any one of which might be something to build on – material, news!) unless they are to be joined by one of his rare visitors, a foreign publisher or translator or some young writer, often American, whose work has attracted him; or, to the consternation of these more serious guests, some odd character whose experience he needs for his work. Not long ago it was a trapeze artist, and earlier a well-known racing driver who was actually photographed with the old man on the terrace, a unique privilege in these later years.

At eleven, whatever the company, bed: the pills on the night table, the glass of water with its lace covering, the pad and pencil, the dark of his mother's bedroom where as a child he had so longed to come and sleep, believing his sleep here, and his dreams, would be different from anything he had experienced in the nursery above. Then darkness, the depths. In which everything is rearranged, reconciled, flickeringly reasserted, seen again in a new light and in a dimension free of the restrictions of time; and where none, not even the dead, are ghosts.

Some of it perhaps will be brought up into the circle of the hooded lamp: odd messages scribbled without his spectacles on the night pad, in a room whose walls surprise him with their whiteness. He will come to the surface, thus, twice or even three times in a single night, to leave these jottings for his daytime self to decipher. But in the early hours he goes deeper,

deeper. No messages from there. Till the first swallows call him up with their distant piping and the light of their tiny bodies dipping through and through the room.

Seven-fifteen, precisely. Like clockwork.

Swallows in their pane of liquid sky and his daughter's discreet tapping at the door.

From the hands of beneficient nature, his taskmaster and nurse, another day.

10

I am standing before the mirror in the office entrance wearing a yellow silk shirt, white trousers *à la* John Travolta and a spotted cravat, which I am just tucking in under the floppy collar.

'You look fine,' Carla says, entering the mirror behind me. 'All you need is – here, lift your chin a little and keep your eyes closed.'

'What are you doing?'

'You'll see.'

She is patting my cheek with her fingertips. I open one eye: her mouth makes a line of concentration, but she is grinning, the grin is in her eyes.

We are about to set off for The Dancing. We have been twice before, on each occasion to one of the gay discos in the centre, which are less likely to attract a purely local clientele; where visitors from out of town turn up, and straight groups who have heard that the gay places are smarter, bigger, better appointed and more uninhibited than the rest. We go separately and do not speak, but understand that we are there as a group. We all have special clothes for these occasions.

'There, you can look now.'

I look. She has heightened the colour of my cheekbones with a touch of make-up and put a dot of it at the corner of my eyes. Somehow it changes the whole shape of my face, emphasizes the darkness of the moustache and sideburns, makes me, I decide, look more aggressively masculine, in the ambiguous style of masculinity that actors project and the models in fashion magazines. Instead of protesting as I might have done a month ago I find myself grinning.

I am supposed to be dour and humourless, and in some ways I am. I am also it seems (or so Carla has disclosed) one of those who will appear at a disco wearing make-up.

I look at myself in this odd fancy-dress and feel extraordinarily liberated. The picture I present, which seems so right for my physical type and generation, is so utterly unlike my real self.

Under cover of my disco clothes I have even discovered a talent for dancing.

'You must be a professional,' a girl tells me, who has been following my steps in a way that suggests that we are, for the moment, partners – but only loosely, and only in passing.

The floor-space of the disco is divided into several dancing areas, some on one level, some on another, with open screenwork between. The varied play of red, blue and green lights over the darkness, together with the regular beat of the music, the constant movement of limbs and the shifting partnerships that are created as single dancers move in and out of the crowd, all this induces a sense of disorientation, as if everything – lights, music, faces, the endless parade of oddly-dressed figures – were part of a private hallucination. It is another sort of cover.

You dance with eyes half-closed from one level to the other, passing from red, through blue, to green; alone, glass in hand, on the lookout, on the move – and this is normal. Or you lean against a column in the broken light of a lattice screen while the colours wash over you, and that too is normal. Using your arms, your hips, you shift in and out of the crowd, allowing the steps themselves to determine which of these strangers will fall for a moment into partnership with you: a boy in a spangled shirt knotted above his navel, another dressed as a sailor – or maybe he is a real sailor – two look-alike cowboys, a girl in leather skirt and boots, another (or is it a boy?) in some sort of forties costume, flared calf-length skirt in watered taffeta, platform sandals, lids thick with mascara under the piled-up hair. The band thumps too loud for conversation. Words are mouthed in the half-dark. People nod and smile or shrug their shoulders as they do a quick turn and swirl away, already involved elsewhere. When the strobe lights play, figures disintegrate under your gaze, all their movements broken up into disjointed fragments with spaces of dark between that your head fits together to make a continuous sequence.

'*I'm* a professional – an actress I mean. I act with the Baccio di Serpente. Have you seen us?'

It is the girl wearing the forties outfit. She *is* a girl,

and tiny, unusually plain, with a bright ugly mouth and a short chin, but when she says again 'I'm an actress' and poses with her right hand open fanwise behind her head, the chin tilted and the face elegantly frozen, I see immediately what she is aiming at; she is beautiful. She gives an ugly grin and goes back to her dislocated shuffling.

'You must come and see us, we're brilliant. Experimental! Audiences hate us. Once we gave a performance for nine hours in an old warehouse, on a stage made of blocks of ice. We just kept saying the same four sentences over and over in different combinations till the ice was melted. Some Fascists threw stones at us, it was sensational. I'm in a new play now where I come on naked and set a table with everything white: white cloth, white napkins, white plastic knives and forks, but very slowly; it takes half an hour. Then I pour out a glass of milk. Then I take everything off again, very slowly, and drink the milk. Then I come on and do it all over again, but this time everything is black, including the milk. I'm brilliant.'

She dances away in her iridescent dress like a vision out of the past, out of the forties, her eyebrows tragically lifted, blowing kisses.

11

The reality of the crime: a condition that is not at all easy to define.

For me it is already real. I have been living the reality of it for the past six weeks. It is the centre round which my day's every act and thought is rigorously organized. Living as I do now I have nothing but the crime to reach out for and touch. It is my only link with the world.

It is to give the crime form and detail, to make it inevitable in the life of the victim, if not in my own, that I spend so many hours poring over all he has ever said and done, over photographs, newspaper cuttings, scholarly articles, and all the rich outpourings of his imagination, to discover, in that dense tapestry of experience and event, the single thread that leads to the Piazza Sant' Agostino and the muzzle of a gun.

The event must have a reality that demands my presence. Not only at the moment of its occurrence but in these long weeks that lead up to it. The crime must have a logic of which that moment in the piazza is the inevitable outcome.

Of course I know that the reality of the crime has a different meaning for the victim. To be alive is one thing, to be dead another. For him the killing has no reality if he is still shuffling about in his worn slippers between desk and bed, sipping coffee, stroking the dog, getting up out of his afternoon nap to make a tiny correction in what he has written – the correction itself a proof of his continuing defiance of that other reality: *Not this word but that other. There, I have added a comma* – pushing forward another page into the 'Work in Progress', the unfinished masterpiece (yes, it will be unfinished) that I too am obsessed by and whose hero I think of as a mirror image of myself, since every move he makes into the fullness of his existence is a move that holds me off.

The 'Work is Progress' is yet another reality. I have begun to search the career of its interesting hero for clues to my own. Does the Master know this? Has he guessed that he is, in a sense, communicating with me? The idea is less fanciful than it appears. Each word he writes now is a word written in defiance of the end, an end he knows may be as close as his next breath. Is it so fantastic that seating himself each morning at the rosewood desk, at precisely the hour that I begin, four hundred kilometres away, to lay out the materials of my research, bringing to the moment all his powers of mind, will, imagination – is it so fantastic that it should be my presence that moves in to fill the nameless, faceless presence, and that the figure he is creating to keep me at a distance should wear my features? He is a magician, and always has been; dealing as much in the purely imaginary as in the world of facts, his mind strangely open at these moments to the flux of things. It is my entry into his time-flow that is being magically excluded by the 'Work in Progress' and by the imposition between us of his hero.

He fascinates me, this hero, this mirror figure whose every step to the right is a step I take to the left, this angel of anti-death. He has no notion as yet of what the end will be. He goes forward, full of boyish charm and vigour and assurance, five hundred words a day, into the open adventure, towards what I know, and the old man must at least accept as a possibility, is the silence at the end of a page. He has no future, this formula-one racing driver and ex-mercenary who in the last episode was preparing, with a touch of colour on his cheeks and a spot of it at the corner of his eyes, to become the mistress – yes, the mistress! – of a Venezuelan oil-magnate.

For it isn't simply death that the 'Work in Progress' defies with its hero's infinite disguises and transformations, his impudent refusal to stay within the bounds of 'character'; it is the author's whole life's work and the pious expectations of his admirers, the notion that he is already dead and done with, a great figure certainly, but one who belongs to the past. Without for a moment losing contact with himself he has turned his own world inside out, remade himself in a form entirely unexpected and unpredictable. He has discovered within him a being who belongs not to old age but to childhood, and not to the end of life but to the fresh, cruel, innocent, destructive beginnings.

Once again I am lost in admiration. How does he do it? How does he manage decade after decade to find this spring in himself that is in touch with the flow, the change, the renewed life of things? Reading through the works one watches him acquire and cast off a dozen different personalities, the jargon of a dozen careers and crafts (all promptly forgotten, he tells us, the moment he has exhausted their use), the modes of a dozen different forms of the 'contemporary'. Is it true, as he has sometimes affirmed, that there are beings among us so finely attuned to the oneness of things that so long as they go with their own nature they are also going with nature herself, are ceaselessly fed, replenished, renewed by her, and cannot take a false step or fail, cannot die even till the natural force of which they are the vehicle chooses some other form for their energy and grants them release?

Knowing what I do of the end I find this idea disturbing. All I have uncovered of the pattern of his life makes me believe, in his case, in the absolute truth of the theory, if only as he makes it true by the ruthlessness of his own will. What then of me? Am I to step in and break the pattern, to act, as it were, against 'nature'? Or am I too part of the natural order of his life?

It is for answers to this question, some clue, perhaps unknown to him, that is hidden in the twists and turns of a fiction that has the savage and beautiful intensity, the impersonal truthfulness, of a child at play, that I read and re-read the 'Work in Progress'. It is, for all its lightness of touch, an extended conversation with

Death. Who can it be addressed to but me?

Realities:

The crime will achieve its final reality at a point long past the moment of its occurrence either in his life or mine; at the point, I mean, when it is reported. The true location of its happening in the real world is not the Piazza Sant' Agostino at P. but the mind of some million readers, and its true form not flesh, blood, bullets, but words: *assassination, brutal murder, infamous crime, mindless violence, anarchy.* Its needing a famous victim and a perpetrator are merely the necessary conditions for its achieving headlines and attracting the words: we are instruments for the transmitting of a message whose final content we do not effect. The crime becomes real because it is reported, because it is called an *act of terrorism*, an *assassination*, because it threatens *mindless violence* and *anarchy*, because it breaks into the mind of the reader as a set of explosive syllables. These are language murders we are committing. What more appropriate victim, then, than our great man of letters? And what more ironical, or more in his line of deadly playfulness, than this subjection of his being to the most vulgar and exploitive terms, this entry into the heart of that reality (that un-reality) that is the war of words.

I am the perpetrator of the infamous crime in the Piazza Sant' Agostino. That it has not yet occurred is neither here nor there. When it does occur it will have no reality till it has been called infamous and the Piazza Sant' Agostino has entered that litany of place names that need no further definition, being each one as clear a term in the continuing argument, the message received and understood, as *terrorist, brutal murder, infamous crime, mindless violence, anarchy.*

Meanwhile I have begun to see my preparation in another light. In entering so completely into his world, in training myself to respond, minute by minute, to the subtle shifts of feeling and sudden bold intuitions that created it, I am fitting myself to become at last one of his characters, the one whose role it is to bring all that fictive creation down about his ears and to present him with his end.

None of this is actually demanded of me. I am called upon only to be his killer. An act of plain butchery, committed by an impersonal representative of the opposing forces, a people's executioner, would meet all the requirements in the strictly historical sense. But I am no longer thinking of history. This is something done for myself; but also, I would like to believe, for him. So that the moment may have some significance beyond what the newspapers will report as meaningless and brutal fact.

12

Walking home last night I realised that the painters on my corner palazzo, my 'clock', have come to the end of this particular job. The open courtyard was full of their pots, brushes, ladders, planks, and I could hear, from one of the upper rooms where the last of them must have been working, the sounds of celebration. I stopped for a moment to listen. Good sounds, those: bits and pieces of singing, sometimes a lone voice, sometimes two or more; laughter; the explosion of a brief friendly scuffle. Later they came down in their dirty overalls, packed the pots, brushes, ladders on to the back of a truck and drove noisily away. Today other workmen, in blue overalls, are dismantling the scaffolding, and as they do so they call across to one another, tease, joke and pause on occasion to follow the progress along the pavement of a pretty girl.

I am sad to have this fragment of bright activity removed from the scene, but it pleases me to think of the decorators, the same team, unloading their equipment this morning and beginning elsewhere. Soon I suppose the removal men will arrive and there will be furniture to watch being hauled up the side of the building or carried, with curses, up the narrow stairs. New children on the street. New early morning shoppers.

Work. I think of my own work suspended all these weeks and waiting to be taken up again when I am freed. It is that that will define me, work among others – the project shared, completed and the new thing taken up. It is beautiful, it carries one on over all the gaps. It is what I most passionately regretted last night when I watched those workmen come stumbling down the stairs together and heard them tease the youngest, the apprentice, with being drunk and incapable as they loaded up, and heard an older man, when he protested, soothe him and say, 'Come on, lad, 'they're only joking. You're alright'.

This is a time outside my life. Like the others I have lent myself to an occasion, a crime, but will be redeemed immediately after. I shall step into this killing and then step out again. On the other side life, and my real life's work.

13

It has happened at last. The group has been disrupted. One of us has been called.

For some reason I had always assumed that I would be the first to go, that I would step away from a group that was still, till I left it, whole and would support me to the last with its wholeness. Not at all.

This morning we took longer than usual to settle ourselves at our desks. We all have our own little habits for getting down to work, as we have habits for preparing ourselves for sleep. Carla takes a great deal of trouble with her chair. She sets and re-sets it, then begins on her lamp. Arturo stacks and re-stacks the new documents he is to deal with till all the edges are even, then places them squarely in the centre of a desk that has been cleared absolutely of every other object. Enzo likes to sit on the desk, with one foot up on his stool, examining his documents a page at a time, lifting only a single corner; then he turns, sits, drops the pages anyhow before him, and holds the backs of hands for a moment against his eyes. This morning we prolonged these activities, each of us waiting for something that was not quite right to right itself before we could begin. At last there was no putting it off any longer. Antonella had not arrived at her usual twenty-four minutes past eight, and she still hadn't arrived at eight-thirty. We set to work in an atmosphere that had been breached. It was as if one whole wall of the apartment had been torn away and was open to grey, slow-moving clouds.

By some odd co-incidence Antonella had arrived yesterday with a bunch of daffodils, which have just begun appearing in the florist's pails, and had set them, six in all, pale yellow trumpets above pale stems, in a tumbler from the kitchen. Flowers are not forbidden exactly – no one has thought to make provision against them – but they are unusual. They sat blaring on Antonella's desk, a reminder; and through their round mouths our lives were suddenly exposed to the spring and its changes, among which Antonella had abruptly disappeared.

Then, just a few minutes late, her key in the lock, and I waited expectantly for her breathless whistling as she hung up her cloak and stopped a moment before the hall mirror to fluff her hair.

Nothing. It was a tall boy with square eyebrows and a beard, his arms half out of a dufflecoat as he introduced himself: 'I'm Angelo.'

We stared. Enzo at last got up and shook the boy's hand, and the rest of us, in a dream, followed.

So it was true. Antonella had been called or replaced. The boy grinned, coughed, looked about to see which of the desks was unoccupied, and we watched as he turned his key, Antonella's key, in the drawer of the filing cabinet. It was empty. Someone had already removed the documents she was working on and everything relating to her.

By mid-morning the newcomer, Angelo, had been absorbed; that is, we had come to terms with the way he filled (with his intense stillness) the gap left by Antonella's everlasting whistling. When the time came to break for lunch he carried off the glass with Antonella's daffodils and set it, very carefully, on the dining room sideboard, a public place where it will no longer cast its shadow on the new set of documents he is at work on and will no longer be Antonella's.

His hands, I notice, are long and thin, with curly black hair on the back of the fingers and grease under the nails. When he eats he holds his knife like a pencil.

A mechanic of some sort, maybe an explosives man. He seems immediately at home among us. It is we who remain disturbed.

Is it always like this, I wonder, the first break in the group, or was Antonella special? Would I miss Carla or Arturo in the same way? I hadn't realized how completely the presence of the others has become part of my sense of myself during these weeks, how much my feeling of wholeness has been this plural existence and inter-dependence of all five. Now that one point of the star has been changed I am changed as well. I have to rethink a whole segment of myself.

Walking home I try to catch a glimpse of the headlines on a newsboard, but it is too soon. We are forbidden to buy papers or listen to the radio or watch TV, though I cheat a little, sometimes, by stopping at a bar to drink coffee while the news plays high up in a corner. Tonight I haven't the daring. I eat quickly and go straight to a movie.

Two girls from nowhere, a blond and a redhead, appear at the side of a motorway and are given a lift by a football team travelling to an away game in another town. Multiple sex on the bus while the highway landscape streams past. More sex in the dressing-room among open lockers; in the showers; in a steam-room with tiled walls. The girls are always naked. The football players wear their boots and a red and white striped jersey, and once one of the girls has a jersey, number 7: the passes and combinations a kind of off-the-field game.

I leave just before the end, take a bus to a quarter on the other side of town and find a girl.

14

I am intolerably restless. The disappearance of Antonella, though I ought to have been prepared for it, continues to disturb me. I know it is meant to happen like this, that she should simply vanish and become one again of the fifty-six million of whom one knows nothing; but it disturbs me just the same, and her replacement by Angelo, the munitions expert, with his thin fingers and lantern jaw, seems too hard a lesson. It is as if the organization had power not only to spirit us away but to transform us as well.

We are all changed by this: the weights between us have been subtly redistributed.

Carla minus Antonella is a lesser woman altogether. The addition of the bomb expert to her character, to her presence even, has shifted some delicate balance that makes her seem suddenly too cool, too hard, has given, by example perhaps, a grimmer line to her jaw and a whip-like emphasis to her gestures that goes beyond precision and makes everything she does seem over-dramatized.

As for Enzo, the removal from the star of one female

point and the introduction of another male one has been too much for him. His hostility to the newcomer is manifest, he cannot control it; and out of irritation with himself for giving so much away, for having in Angelo's case made a distinction, he has increased his hostility to Arturo and me as well. Mealtimes are aglow with tension, with palpable silences in which the bomb expert works his jaw, chewing every mouthful twenty times and leaving the sticky print of his fingers over everything he touches, quite unaware of what he has done to us.

He is, most of all, the one among us who has never known Antonella; that is what makes him so deeply a stranger. There is a whole side of us that he will never understand. Soon, I suppose, we will have to think of the group as reconstituted and take him into our lives as we took her, but somehow I don't fancy the aspects of myself that he might call into being. Why, I wonder? Is it the grease? That visible sign that we are not, after all, dealing entirely with abstracts, we clean-fingered intellectuals, but with a world in which reality has another shape and smell altogether?

There are also his long absences in the Signora's bedroom, where he is constructing a 'device'. At any moment, should those slim fingers make an error, we might be blown to smithereens. *That* is the shape of reality.

I must be chosen next. It angers me that I adjust so slowly. If Carla were to go now, or even Enzo or Arturo, I might break completely.

And that too is the 'shape of reality'.

15

Yesterday, for the first time, I had an encounter with one of my neighbours. The whole thing was simple enough, and might have been expected, but has added to my sense of unease. Another breach in my perfect isolation from the world about me.

Each of the various rooms and apartments in the palace has a post-box in the courtyard with a switch that lights the stairs above. I was making my way up beyond the first floor when I heard a whimpering to my right and then a faint voice: 'Please, whoever it is, I am here in the dark.'

I took a step or two into the corridor and hesitated. Better really not to get involved, to ignore the voice and go on.

'Please. I can't find my way up or down.' The voice was old and urgent. 'I can't sit here all night.'

It was just after six and still perfectly light outside, but on the stairway above as black as midnight.

'I've been here for hours.'

I took three or four paces along the corridor and realized I was at the foot of yet another stairway. The voice was immediately above. I took out my lighter. Half-sitting, half-sprawled on the stairs was an old woman in black, her shawl pushed back off her head, a brown-paper bag in her arms that had already split and spilled some of its contents: two lemons, a frozen chicken on a plastic tray, a head of lettuce. I knelt to gather them up and she grasped my hand with a strength that surprised and alarmed me.

'You won't leave me.'

'Of course not.' I took the paper bag, put the fallen articles back inside and drew it together as well as I could. 'Is it up here?'

'Yes. I got halfway up but the lights went out, the bulb must have blown. I couldn't see where I was. I tried to come down again,' she suddenly burst into tears, 'and fell.'

'Well, let's try again. I'll use my lighter.'

I soon lost all sense of what part of the palace we were in as we climbed stairway after stairway. 'Yes, yes,' she prompted me, 'to the right. Now left. We're almost there. Now the stairway at the end. I'm sorry to be so slow, but I'm old you know. Seventy-seven, and Celeste is eighty-two. I've lived here for fifty-four years. I came as a bride.' I had stopped and turned, holding the lighter high so that she could see her way, and she must have caught the look in my eyes, 'Oh yes,' she said, time goes fast enough,' as if fifty years were no more than the little space of darkness between us. She was holding up her key. We had come to the door. I stood back, with the parcel awkwardly in one hand and the lighter in the other so that she could open it.

'I'm coming, Celeste,' she called as she stooped to the keyhole, 'I'm coming, my darlings. I was lost on the stairs, but a kind young man has brought me back.'

We were in a good-sized vestibule. I suppose I had expected a cupboard like my own room, so the size of the entrance, its height, the oriental rugs, the mirror in its gilded frame, surprised me. 'Come,' she said, and turned left through a set of double doors into a sitting-room that must, I realized, run the whole length of the palace above the square. Its long windows with their gauze curtains and velvet drapes were filled with the western light off the river, a muted gold.

I had never seen a room like it. Every available space was filled with birdcages of every shape and size, squares, hexagons, spheres, some like pagodas, others again like mosques; all the birds chirping and shrilling and rolling and fluttering their coloured wings against the bars. I stood there, hugging my parcel with its one frozen chicken, and was dizzy with it all, the colour, the noise. Some of the birds in the cages, I now saw, were stuffed; and there were birds of more exotic varieties, with scarlet or bright blue wings, on the mantelpiece and under glass domes on table-tops. Coming in out of the dark maze of the stairway was like stumbling suddenly into a jungle clearing. Except for the clocks. There were also clocks: tall grandfathers in walnut and mahogony, inlaid or plain, with painted dials and wheels, chains, pendulums; slim grandmothers suspended; standing pieces in gilt and porcelain, their globes supported by naked nymphs or eighteenth-century shepherds; carriage clocks, water-clocks, clocks with a mechanism that went up and down like a sewing-machine needle, all ticking and tinkling. It was, I decided later, the mixture of shrill birdsongs and the unsynchronized ticking and chiming of the clockworks that most unnerved me – I couldn't imagine what kind of collector could have mixed them all up like this, the alive and the mechanical. It seemed profoundly crazy. And the thought that it had been here all along, just metres away from my own room, changed the whole place for me. The plainness of my cell seemed violated by the proximity.

The old woman had simply disappeared.

But was there, after all, behind a Chinese screen that was also covered with birds, made of *papier mâché* but stuck all over with natural feathers.

'Please,' she called, 'sit down somewhere, and make yourself at home. I'll be with you' – she paused and seemed to be lifting a heavy weight – 'in just a minute.'

She emerged wheeling another old woman in a chair.

'This is my sister-in-law, Celeste. Signora Carola, my husband's sister.' She took the parcel from me, looked about, frowned, and finally set it down under a sofa table.

'This is the young man who rescued me, Celeste. I'm about to give him a drink.'

The old woman in the chair made no sign of understanding.

She poured a glass and handed it to me. 'Poor

Celeste, she doesn't hear. But I feel it is mean not to tell her things. There! Your health! She does hear sometimes, I think. At least the birds. They're hers, you know, and the clocks were my husband Ugo's, he collected them from all over, England, the United States, Hungary. I've always hated them, and to tell you the truth, I don't care much for the birds either – I call them my darlings out of habit, for her sake. They have to be fed special kinds of seed and their cages have to be cleaned – a terrible business! You wouldn't believe what they manage to drop, those tiny creatures, in spite of the singing. Especially now that Pia doesn't come. Pia came even after we couldn't really pay her any more, but she's dead now, and her daughter came once or twice but couldn't bear the birds, so she stopped. I understand that. She didn't mean to be unkind. At least the clocks don't need to be fed or cleaned up after. But they do need winding. I hate the noise they make, but I couldn't bear it if they stopped and just sat there with all their works going to rust. So you see what my life is. I'm needed every minute. I go out only to get food . . .'

Outside in the dark of the stairway at last I began the difficult process of finding my way back to the point where my own stairway led off to the other side of the courtyard. It must have taken me nearly a quarter of an hour of false turnings and experimental steps along deserted corridors before I arrived at the wide passageway on the first floor. All this in absolute silence. The doors I passed were closed, and no sound penetrated their solid timber. They were all double-barred with that peculiar system of rising rods that is used against unwanted intruders. You see people standing at a door, turning their keys, once left, twice right, and listening for the mystical rising and falling within of the oiled machinery.

This glimpse into the life beyond one of those doors has thrown the whole palace into a new light. I had thought of my own room as hanging up there detached and in darkness, arrived at by its own set of stairways and utterly sealed off. Now it is part of a system that also contains, just below and to the right, on the other side of the courtyard, that room filled with clocks and songbirds, and the two old women.

I think of this encounter as being the first of my 'dreams' – a dream that I cannot interpret. The fact is that till then my nights in that little box of a room had been mostly dreamless, as if my sleep reflected the blankness of its walls, the absence from it of all but the most essential objects, and even those, as far as possible, impersonal. These last nights have been not troubled exactly, but coloured by extraordinary fantasies. I remember nothing afterwards, but the slight sweat on my skin when I wake, a lingering light behind the eyes that is not of this season, or this hemisphere, suggest that I have been off in exotic places and have undergone unusual and unsettling adventures. An element of the unpredictable, that for weeks now I have kept deeply submerged, has forced its way to the surface. I am unwilling at times to lie down, turn off the light and expose myself to the vagaries, sometimes savage, sometimes I suspect merely ridiculous, of my own imagination.

I begin to understand a little what the Master calls 'The anti-Works'.

16

A dream:

I have brought no detail out of the dark; only the mood of it that still colours the edge of everything about me, a weather I find myself moving in all day.

No mere recounting of the events of a dream can reproduce for us the peculiar quality of its light or the emotion it floods us with; the events are nothing. So if I am to describe it now it cannot be through any reference to the dream itself. I shall describe instead a photograph I discovered recently in an old book, which has been taken in just such a light and whose figures – or perhaps it is simply their disposition in the frame – evoke for me the mood of what I dreamt, though I have erased completely its sequence of phantom events.

It is afternoon in the early twenties. On the rocks of a little cove, with a low headland beyond and a path across it that leads perhaps to a village, five figures are waiting for a boat. The light comes over the smooth water from the direction in which they are gazing; there are big rocks made jagged with sun and shadow, and smaller rocks that barely break the ripples, on one of which, far out to the left of the photograph and completely surrounded by water, a girl is standing. She wears a silk dress in the flat-chested, beltless style of the period; it is dark with white spots. Her head is contained in a tight cloche, her hands are clasped below her waist and she is leaning backward a little to keep her balance, so that you are aware of the tension behind the knees and the effort it must take to keep her small feet firmly planted in the low-cut, strapped and buttoned shoes.

Deeper in the photograph, immediately behind her, a pleasant, well-knit young man is seated on one of the largest rocks of all, looking very casual in rolled shirt-sleeves. His collar has been unbuttoned and his tie hangs in a deep loop. One leg is comfortably raised to provide a rest for his elbow. His face is in profile. He too, like the girl, is looking towards the source of light, but her figure, in its tenseness, suggests that the boat is already in sight, she is prepared for embarkation and departure; he is still resting lazily in the sun, he sees nothing as yet. They might be present at different events.

Behind the girl again, but closer to the foreground, so that the lower part of his body is hidden by rocks, is an older man (nearing forty) in a cloak, or a topcoat drawn loosely about his shoulders. He wears a white panama with the brim turned down, round spectacles and a floppy cravat. His elbows are bent, his hands joined; he might be holding a ticket. His cloak suggests some other season than the one the girl has prepared for in her light silk dress, or the one the young man has loosened his tie and rolled his shirtsleeves to enjoy the warmth of. He belongs to another period, another class, another mode of life. What boat, one wonders, could be stopping off here to take all three of these passengers aboard? What journey could they be taking in common?

Higher up the shoreline, behind the formal stranger, stands another girl. She is wearing the same kind of clothes and shoes as the first, but everything about her is heavier, darker – and it isn't simply that she is further from the left-hand side of the photograph which is so brightly suffused with sunlight. The thick plait over her shoulder, her stance, the strap bag that takes the weight of her bent arm, her flesh – all these are dark; she is standing in the light of a different occasion, so that her face can barely be seen, and she is looking not out to sea, in the direction of the picture's expected action, but has half-turned, as if momentarily distracted, to where, behind us, some other event is in process, some other conveyance has appeared. (Is it a fishing-boat? A space-ship?) She is younger than the others, she might be seventeen, and the shape of her face – she is too deep in shade to have features – suggests that she is extraordinarily pretty.

There is one other figure. Seated a little apart from the rest, on the rocks at the far right of the photograph, and facing dead ahead so that his face is in shadow, is a young peasant. He wears a suit, a tie, a flat tweed cap, and he sits with his forearms extended along his thighs. Only the big fists are in full sunlight. The grain of the material in the flat cap that is set straight on his brow, in the jacket that fits tight over the square shoulders, is so clear that you could pick out the threads; but his face is in total darkness and his fists are a blaze.

There is nothing in the photograph, save perhaps the isolation of the figures from one another, that could account for the immense sadness it fills me with. The sun is shining, the afternoon sky makes the pale sea shimmer. It is a sadness that seems inevitable, and to be in the very nature of things. Fifty years ago it had these five strangers looking, at this moment, towards the arrival of a boat that may or may not have appeared, that may or may not be making towards the rocks of the little cove, out of a future that has, for long years now, been no more than a moment in the past. They seem just close enough to look like contemporaries, and just distant enough to be touched with the unlikeliness of those who belong already to history. I find myself fingering the surface of the photograph and being surprised that the rocks are not jagged, that the roughness of that boy's jacket, which the light inside the photograph makes so real, cannot be felt.

My dream stands in the same relationship to me as the photograph. It teases me with the deepest and most physical sense of space, light, weather, of the various textures of things, of a huge and inevitable sadness, but when I try to enter its reality I cannot. Is this what the dead feel?

17

There are times, in spite of our orders, when it is difficult to shut out the news. A few words overheard in the bus are like the turning of a shocking page.

Another nest discovered and the terrorists taken with all their documents – any one of which, together with a hundred other seemingly unrelated facts, might throw up as in a puzzle, where it needs only the slightest rearrangement of the coloured squares to produce a pattern that is instantly recognizable, a name, a face.

Or a shoot-out in a suburban apartment. A quiet corridor in the middle of the night runs red with blood. One, two, five bodies, called up without warning out of the depths of sleep, fully armed but dressed only in underpants and singlet or in the briefest slip, go down in a storm of bullets before any one of them can pull the pin on a grenade or fire off a single shot, stepping straight out of the warmth and safety of sleep into their own blood.

All this one must imagine from facts picked up here and there between talk about hair-styles, boyfriends and last night's television programmes – gossip from the front, filled out with newspaper headlines on windy boards and images it is better not to look at, flickering high up in the corner of a bar or repeated five times over, in sickening colour, on the display sets in shop windows.

This, three days after Antonella's disappearance, is how I hear of the gun-battle at T.

Three comrades caught in a car and surrounded, all three killed. The driver instantly, shot at the wheel; the other man in a brief exchange of gunfire from behind the door of the vehicle; the girl in a side street as she tries to get away, sprawling in the gutter with her skirt up over one thigh and a shoe missing.

There are pictures. They are terribly distorted, the figures already dissolving as they move quickly on out of life. With their edges frayed, great holes for eyes, they have been endowed with a fuzzy insubstantiality, a flat black-and-white quality that marks them as figures from the news, fighters at the edge of history who have, as it were, broken up in casting themselves against solid print.

Newspaper photography.

Far from catching life it disintegrates and dissolves it, first reducing it to a pattern of tiny dots and areas of patchy light and dark, then recreating it to make an image we recognize but no longer feel related to, something that belongs to 'the news', and in entering that utterly flat dimension relinquishes its right to be considered real.

Of course the acts we produce have significance

only if they are reported. But the very fact of their being reported changes them. As they pass into the public domain they lose whatever they had of flesh and blood and acquire that deadness, that finality, that impersonal and isolating distance that belongs to what has been given over to the tense of retelling: to history, to death. There is no way out of this dilemma. We can only work through a medium which is itself the enemy and whose very nature is to deprive whatever it reports of life and power.

One sees this most clearly when a cache of weapons is pictured on the same page as a group of comrades, either alive or dead. They look so solid, those Lugers, Skorpions, Smith and Wessons, grenades, anti-tank missiles, all laid out neatly in rows. It is the human figures that break up in the mind, that fail to hold their form. It is difficult, even with a real name supplied, to imagine that any of these figures might once have been more than what the pictures reduce them to, such obvious outsiders, rebels, misfits that you wonder how they ever went unrecognized in the streets.

No resemblance at all between Graziella da Soto, aged 20, Chilean, and the Antonella whose bubbly music so often distracted me and set my fingers tapping on the desk. These blank eye-sockets, these luminous cheeks, this raw mouth.

But it is her, it must be.

Graziella.

I buy a paper, take it back to my room and sicken myself with it, devouring every line.

Next day I am inclined to believe that I am the only

one of us who has cheated. But it is soon clear from the atmosphere as we set to work that the others are also dealing this morning with the huge clamour of Antonella's disintegration under the fire of five plain-clothes policemen in an ambush. The office is full of the sudden rackety burst of the machine-guns – five seconds of utter bedlam over and over in the silence of our skulls; and the flesh is solid enough to feel the impact, however subtly in the photographs it may suggest nothing more than light dots and dark. Only our mechanic seems unaware that we are in turmoil here, that all the conditions of our relationship to one another have once again been changed, and that some part of us still echoes with unresolved possibilities as the bullets tear through it in a last moment of consciousness.

Again next day the papers are full of it. More theories, different facts, but the same pictures.

I turn away from my neighbours on the bus and for the first time feel anger and disgust to see the dirty black print that comes off on their hands, on their eyes too, as they rub themselves against the obscene paragraphs. I stay out of the bars. I eat at home. One more day perhaps and something new will have arisen to wipe Antonella off the newsboards and the lips of the commuters – a plane-crash, a bribery scandal. She will remain in the public files, every detail of her existence lovingly recorded and remembered, and in the heads of Carla, Arturo, Enzo and me; and I see now that we will always be part of one another and will always feel the absence of the others, in whatever form, as the aching of a phantom limb. I had not seen that till now. I find in myself a kind of tenderness, even for Enzo, who seems 'nobler' and more hostile than ever in this new light, and for Arturo too, who has had his hair cut and looks unbearably school-boyish. As for Carla, I dare not look at her. One glance between us and our whole lives might fly apart.

On my way home I stop in the cold and watch some children playing in the square, small muffled figures flying about over the gravel between the trees; one of them always the outsider, the others always in flight from him, but their cries, their trails of white breath, mingling and the outsider always managing at last to touch one of his comrades and so break back into the group.

I watch for ten minutes the ever-changing pattern with its simple rule, and for all that time am intensely absorbed and happy, caught up in the energy of those hot little bodies in their swinging away from whoever it is that is momentarily 'he', as the ambiguous gift of singularity, like a curse or infection, passes from one to another and they find themselves in flight from a different centre, throwing their slight weight off now in a fresh direction and leaving behind always, under the wet branches, the quick-fading white of their breath.

18

On my desk this morning, along with a new instalment of the 'Work in Progress' and two articles on the Master from American magazines (one on water as a regenerative symbol in his novels, the other a painful attempt to define his political attitudes) a cutting from one of the provincial papers. Three brief paragraphs.

They announce the death, in a clinic at P., of Signora Dora Cavani.

A well-known figure in the years between the wars, though now largely forgotten, she was, it seems, the friend, patroness and correspondent of some of the most famous artists of the century – among them, in a list that includes Stravinski, De Chirico, Saba, Pound, Pavese and Kurt Schwitters, our author. She has been in a coma, kept alive by a life-support system, for the past six weeks, and is to be buried from the Church of Sant' Agostino at three-thirty on Tuesday afternoon.

So there it is: the day, the time. The jigsaw is complete. Tucked away in the announcement of a death in a provincial paper, the final piece.

I read the cutting a dozen times over and can hardly believe it.

From the very beginning one of the puzzles to me has been how our people could be certain that the great man, who goes nowhere these days, never leaves the house or breaks his routine, would appear in the piazza for his own assassination.

But there was never any doubt of it. The thread we have been hanging on all these weeks was the woman's life. Laid out there between white walls in the clinic at P., it was her shallow breathing that determined the time-span of our operations, and her feeble heartbeat, sustained by a machine whose little wheels turned night and day and whose needle recorded, under the eyes of anxious monitors, her fragile hold on her own life, that held me off and kept him safe.

I had often conceived of some secret link between us as we sat absorbed in our different tasks; he at the big desk above the fields, in a room still coloured by the light of his dreams, I at my table in the apartment; isolated, alone, and with four hundred kilometres and a lifetime between us, but gathered in the same fateful design.

Now, in retrospect, I must add another to the picture: the woman – prone, gaunt, flat-chested, her mouth slightly open to take in air; and beyond even her, the machine to which all three of us were obscurely connected, its metal surfaces softly agleam as it marked its own time in the dark.

It makes another pattern altogether, and I should

have learned nothing in these long weeks of immersing myself in his world of delicate distinctions and balances if I did not feel, at this moment, how clumsy a third I make, intruding so crudely, armed only with a cause and cold steel, on a relationship that has been sustained with so much tact, and such high feeling on both sides, for more than half a century. I am abrupt, accidental. She has been, for all that long stretch of time, the keystone of his existence.

Dora Cavani.

The name echoes and re-echoes in his papers. There are nearly a thousand letters to her, from Switzerland and Argentina during his exile, from his travels all over the Mediterranean in the thirties – vivid, hastily scribbled postcards or deep meditations, one or two even from the days when he was a student in Milan, before his gift had reached out and claimed him. They are not passionate; she was, after all, happily married to another man. But he dedicated a volume of essays to her, and she has sometimes been thought to be the model for Renata in an early story of first love, though the story's hero is his brother. (Is there a clue there to something deeper than he has ever confessed?) It has been suggested that his return to P., twelve years ago, may be linked with her retirement there on the death of her husband. She is certainly the Dear Friend he so often apostrophises in the later essays, the last survivor of an earlier world with whom he can share his memories, and through whose sympathy and affection so much of it comes back to him – as he has put it, 'another patch of blue'. Is she also, perhaps, the

Dearly Beloved whose identity the commentators have never established but whose presence he so often evokes as Guide and Muse, the one true love he has never outgrown? Was it her presence at P., rather than the recovery of his own deepest roots of family, place, language, that let him through again into his earliest childhood – or are the two things, as he felt them, indistinguishable?

A long passage in the *Memoir* describes an accidental return to the district, and a walk from the farmhouse where he had grown up to the house of an early love, an hour off over the hills. The walk, as so often with him, immediately becomes symbolic, and the more so as he notes, rock by rock, leaf by leaf, each landmark along the way, re-entering, as it were, the strong net of feelings that for years had lain over these objects. Having for so long retained their power, they now, as he approaches, release it again as if nothing had changed: a line of poplars along a fence, all the trunks black, the leaves bright gold; five stepping stones over a stream, the third of which is not quite firm – and just as he had remembered after nearly sixty years, it tilts underfoot; a lilac bush in a clump of ferns. All the feelings inherent in the landscape come back with instant force, but he understands them now as he had failed to understand before. It is his younger self who stands looking back across the whole stretch of his life, and his younger self who starts breathlessly up the slope towards the house, where the young girl still stands under the jasmine bush at the end of the path, though it is – O happy rediscovery! – an older woman who turns and makes towards him.

So he found his way back, he tells us, to the beginning, 'a full circle to the place where I began.'

I had assumed all this was only half true: a grain of actuality – how large no one could tell – the rest an elaboration. It had seemed too deeply stained with poetry to be true to the events.

But there is a poetry of events after all. Think of what is now to occur. It makes a pattern he would recognize and approve as being very much his own. A touch more melodramatic, that death on the steps after the Beloved's funeral, than he might allow himself in fiction, but as true to the real shape of his life as anything he could have imagined, an ending that richly justifies everything he has ever claimed for himself. Mightn't he even, in some obscure way, have chosen it? Or imagined it deep within him and then used his extraordinary powers to bring it about?

And what part do I play in all this? Might I, facing him on the steps of the piazza, revolver in hand, be just what he had already foreseen? And I don't mean the assassin of Santo Domingo. Or if I do, I mean him only as a shadow of what we might both be: the brother fallen in battle nearly sixty years ago and returning at last to claim his life, the son with his rifle, who aims at some distant object, then, with a knowing smile, turns it squarely upon himself, and for a second time finds his father's heart. Will he meet me as a figure entirely known and expected? – 'Ah yes, it is you. I should have guessed.' – conjured up in the piazza, at the last moment, out of his need to complete the business after his own wishes and in his own style.

It occurs to me that I will only make sense of all this by going back to the works themselves and reading them through again from first to last. Somewhere in the slow unfolding of his life in time is the pattern this new piece of evidence may reveal to me. I need to see that pattern. Not for what it will explain of our author, or the mysterious wholeness and poetry of his life, but to discover what I am doing here and whose destiny it is I have been summoned to fulfil.

But there is no time. I have been handed this last piece of the jigsaw when it is too late to use it. I will enter the piazza as the figure in this drama who knows least of all what it really means. My researches were for nothing. I had the evidence before me but did not know what I was looking for. I was looking for *him.* I ought all the time to have been seeking myself.

19

It has come. Returning to my room this evening I had the clear sensation, before I had even felt for the switch, that its order had been disturbed. There on the table, the only surface in the room that wasn't perfectly bare, lay a squat, brown-paper parcel. I stood mesmerized before it.

It was shapeless, and might have contained anything: a spanner or a child's tip-truck or a shaving kit. A moment later, with no memory of having untied the string or unfolded the three thicknesses of paper, I was holding in my hand, and so easily that I might have handled this thing every day of my life, a ·765 Beretta automatic.

I had asked myself many times how the order would arrive. I suppose I expected a knock on the door and a face, a voice at last, someone who might put his hand on my shoulder and offer a few words of gentle reassurance – I wouldn't have had to believe them, the voice would be enough – maybe wish me luck even or make some kind of awkward joke.

Not at all. The angel of this annunciation is black,

cold, and fits snugly into the hand.

No need for words. The object is itself the message. I have known from the beginning that when the sign is made I must present myself at a certain place at a certain time and wait to be picked up.

So it is fixed. These last weeks are already done with. I am turned in the direction of what my life is to be from now on. But before that, there is the brief detour to the Piazza Sant' Agostino at P.

Now that it has come I feel light-headed and suddenly very tired. I lay the weapon down, without bothering to rewrap it or make any other preparations, stretch full length on the bed and immediately fall into a profound sleep.

Total blackness, as if I had been drugged.

When I wake hours later the light is still on. The clock says five minutes to three. I lie staring at the ceiling, and for the first time since the wrappers revealed the shiny glint of it, my mind begins working again and my heart suddenly thumps and races. I go quickly to the table. It is there: utterly itself. Black, weighty, its clean lines, with the inviting grip, so beautifully attuned to its purpose that the purpose itself seems like nature; it is as if such an object had existed from the first moment of creation, and the hand, its four fingers and flexible thumb, had grown to fit it, the two shapes, hand and pistol, developing in perfect parallel with one another to reach their perfected forms.

Only my hand is shaking too badly at the moment to take it up. I bite my lip, clench my fists at the table edge, wait for my blood to settle. When my hand is steady I reach out for it. The grip of the thing, its balance, its coolness, has a soothing effect, such as I might have expected from that reassuring voice, for which it is after all the impersonal substitute. I stand in the centre of the room and hold it easily just at waist level. I have regained that unconscious, almost dream-like self that unwrapped the parcel and let the gun settle so snugly into place. That is how it must be later. As it is now.

Meanwhile there are preparations to make.

I wash and change my clothes, then arrange my few possessions in a haversack. I do all this very slowly, very carefully, to fill the time; and discover that for the past ten minutes or more I have been talking aloud though I can't recall a word that has been said. When everything is neatly done, and every last trace of my presence has been removed from the room, I sit on the bed and wait.

The room contains no trace of me.

I remove myself from it.

An hour later I start awake where I have sunk back against the wall, perfectly alert and clear-headed, fully dressed even to the jacket, and with the haversack, in which the gun is hidden, already over my shoulder. It is after four.

Now begins the worst of it. I have nothing to do but wait. I am not required for several hours yet, but here I am with my whole life on my hands and a mind that has thrown off weariness and the first shock that laid me out like a hammerblow, and is simply with me now as it always is, a machine with a life of its own and all the past available in its memory banks to be called as needed, and set for a future it never doubts for a moment is there. The mind imposes itself. It too has to be taken along and out through the event. Meanwhile I would give anything for some fact or puzzle with which it might occupy itself and leave me free . . .

I find I have been talking aloud again, and again there is no record in my memory of the conversation; or if there is I cannot locate it. Maybe it will reappear later, in what I have already set my course for, and want now with a passionate longing – that ordinary life that lies just a few hours ahead, on the far side of the event.

Yes, I tell my father, as if picking up the threads of a broken conversation, *I do mean to marry. Yes, grandchildren. Your grandchildren. Mine.*

My body knows them, those future generations as if the years to come lay vividly before me and they were already flesh and blood, filling the silence with their voices. I would like to call out to them, but have forgotten their names.

I wish you were here, I say. *I want so much at this moment to talk to you, to let my mind idle on the vibrations of your voice, to have that set the tone of these last moments in the room.*

And realize, with a little shock, that it isn't my father I am addressing but *him.*

Is he stirring already out of the shallow sleep of the old? Turning towards the first light of dawn that I can see colouring the window, pushing a foot down into the colder reaches at the bottom of the bed, snuffling, hauling the rug up over his hunched shoulder, rising slowly towards the surface, the few pints of thin blood still pumping, the viscera tightly packed under the wrinkled belly, still miraculously intact after another night out there in the no-man's-land of sleep? This, I feel, might be the moment. Just now in the lightness of his early morning sleep, when the mind looks two ways, we might make contact at last and the conversation take place that I long for as one might long for forgiveness. It is after all *words* that I need. I feel so utterly alone, so vulnerable to things: to the little waterdrops that will be hanging on the bare twigs of trees in the square below, little swellings of early light where next month there will be blossom; to the children with their pale cries that I stood and watched playing tag in the square, who will be deep now in the sleep of early childhood or making those fabulous excursions out of themselves that are children's dreams; to the cats scavenging for scraps in cold doorways; to the shallow pools of rain in the gravel walks that will be dry by midday, their drying up a process of forgetting, drop by drop, the passage of the new moon across them; to the grains of soot that settle on treetrunks and boughs, leaving them streaked with dew; to the round lids of manholes that are stamped with the city's ancient insignia – a blind eye turned downward into the bowels of the city, whose odours clog it with rust; to the light that slowly advances out of the darkness of things, out of leaves, stones, pools, scraps of paper, out of hands and faces, out of the depths of space itself, and which cannot be resisted as it pours out endlessly, endlessly, giving each thing shape, colour, solidity, making reality something that knocks against all five senses to prove us real. At this point of powerful weakness, of openness to the common life of things, surely we might at last make contact.

I feel him turn once more. He is at the very edge of wakefulness now, but troubled still by the tail of a dream that detains him down there, though the small sounds of morning are already providing the threads on which he will rise and break surface.

His hand goes out to the waterglass on the night table with the pills beside it. *Why am I thinking of that young man – that seminarist, Francesco, who killed the ambassador at Santo Domingo? Why after all this time has he come back to tug at me? I've said all I had to say about him, or for him. All I knew.* In this odd moment between sleep and waking he almost catches sight of me, might still, if he could grasp the fading vision at the corner of his eye – *that young man, was it? at the tramstop in Zurich* – see me here as he sits up and swings his legs over the side of the bed, with his bluish feet not yet thrust into the black kid slippers. *I have woken early.*

I wait, listening. The thin lips move. The head nods over its thought, or perhaps simply because its weight is no longer quite controllable. But there is no word. In a moment his daughter will appear, place a dedicatory kiss on his brow, express surprise that on this of all days – later, in the afternoon he has an appointment – he has beaten the clock and stirred early. Yes, there is her tap at the door.

She leaves his coffee on the tray and goes into the next room. As he sips and takes a bite from his English water-biscuit he consults the pad that stands beside the glass of water and reads the scribblings that have emerged out of his broken sleep, the night-thoughts that offer the merest, most fascinating glimpse – just the end of a page tantalizingly lifted – of 'the anti-Works', those shadows, volume by volume, of what he has brought into the light. No clue there. What was it that was haunting him? *What? What?*

I am already fading from view. The possibility will pass. He is already engaged, his mind suddenly active in one of the scribblings. He adds something. Crosses a word out and adds two more. Is it some thought to be discovered on the nightpad that gives his mouth that little twist as he takes another sip from the cup, or just the bitterness of the coffee, which he takes without sugar? *Ah, the world is so strange, so sad! But interesting!*

Too late now. He has already abandoned me. If there was a point, back there, when his mind, not yet grounded in actualities and particulars, was adrift among the infinite possibilities and still open for any one of them to enter or be entered, it has passed. His working day has begun.

He puts the coffee aside, still unfinished, and scribbles rapidly, making a little chuckling sound. His eyes brighten. Another fragment of darkness has been brought out into the world of grace and light.

These are the only words that emerge. I cannot read them.

It is seven-thirty. The water is still running for his bath. I go out quickly without looking at the room where I have spent nearly six weeks of my life, close the door softly, descend the stairs, pass the corridor that leads to my old lady with the clocks, which will be ticking away now as they set out across the morning, and the caged birds in the dark of their covers, not yet pricked into song.

I cross the square. It is empty, except for a tramp curled up as usual in the doorway of the florist's. I turn into the avenue, walk briskly to the corner and then run the last twenty metres.

I am on my way.

20

It is over, and nothing has gone as planned.

The car, when it pulled in under the archway where I had been instructed to wait, was a delivery wagon with a girl at the wheel, a girl with sleek black hair that curled outwards under her ears. It was only when I climbed in beside her and she turned to smile at me that I recognized her. Carla! How different the change of hair colour made her. I opened my mouth to speak, but before I could do so she introduced herself.

'I'm Adriana. I'm to drive you. I am also your cover. It isn't forbidden, but it would be better if we didn't speak.'

We drove out of the narrow street into a wider one, then out along one of the viales, and within minutes the town, all its church towers picked out in the early sunlight, was hovering below, caught in gaps between the trunks of pines.

I glanced sideways once at her profile and she tilted her head a little and gave me a clear indication that that too, though it wasn't exactly forbidden, might be better avoided. I watched the town, which I had never really got to know in my five weeks there, sink away between the rough-textured pink and brown trunks – its great dome, its famous galleries with all the paintings at this hour still in darkness behind locked doors, its river spanned by elegant stone bridges. But at last it was gone and there were stone walls close on either side, with just a glimpse of olive-groves or orchards on the rises and Carla's unfamiliar profile under the black wig.

It disturbed me to know that the girl beside me had once stepped into my sleep and played a part there that I could never quite recall, though my body remembered, with a rising warmth, the mood of it. Had she been dark-haired then as well? It seemed to me now that she had, and that it was this, rather than anything we had said or done, that had embarrassed me in the days afterwards when I met her eyes across the dining table; as if I had hit upon some aspect of her in my sleep that she might not be aware of, or had long kept hidden, as she once, and quite consciously, had brought out some hidden side of me, when standing before the mirror in the apartment she had touched my cheeks with make-up and put those little dots of scarlet at the corners of my eyes. Now here she was just as I had imagined her. Or had my dream itself been changed in recollection by her new appearance? Our relationship has always, it seems, been closer than we knew. Week after week we have been engaged on the same material, covering one another in secret, working side by side in separation but endlessly crossing tracks. Is that why I dreamed of her, and so precisely as she now appeared? Not blond Carla, but Carla Adriana in a black wig. And what, I wondered, given my own involvement, was her relationship with our famous victim? What aspects of herself had she been following in the vast mirror-world of his writings and how was her part in it related to mine? Once again it occurred to me that I needed to read the whole works through again, this time seeking her, my understudy, my double in another form.

She turned her head once or twice to observe me. (Had I been talking aloud?) And this time it was I who obeyed the rules.

'We've got about four hours of this,' she said, as we pulled away from the toll-gate on the highway. 'You should try to sleep.'

I might have protested then that I had slept enough, and was already in what seemed to myself to be too trance-like a state for what lay ahead. But her words, spoken I thought later as one might speak to a small child, had the effect on me of a hypnotic command. Perhaps it was the warmth of the cabin and the protective closeness of her presence: perhaps it was simply the steady motion of the vehicle, or my own wish to be released for a time from my condition of questioning anxiety; but almost immediately I began to lose consciousness, felt her settle a cushion under my head, and fell into a blankness that only gradually lightened, after I don't know how long, to reveal a long flat stretch of beach in what I recognized as Southern California. It was mid-afternoon. Fog lay over the ocean, but the beach and the very edge of the sea were in sunlight. Small clean waves fell over themselves on the glassy sand, and half a dozen riders were urging their horses through them, the horses, with highlights shifting on their flanks, tall and dark against the sky, the riders straight and tall, but faceless. Their voices urged the horses on with clouds of white; and slowly, one after another, the horses turned seaward, waded out with the strange light on their flanks and were lost in fog. And it was as if I were one of those horses; or maybe a rider who had slipped from his horse far out. Warm water was all about me but I was in fog. There was no sign of the shore and no indication out there of where it might lie or in which direction I should strike out towards it. The water was thick and warm, and I had the sick sensation that if the fog were to lift and light fell upon it, it would be red. I struggled and it began to thicken, my limbs were clogged. I worked my legs and shoulders, I tried to cry out, and the air in my lungs was raw and cold. I tried again, and this time my throat was filled with sound. A cry spun out. It was a lifeline I could grasp, hold and climb out on.

I blinked awake. We had come to a halt.

'You were having a bad dream,' Carla Adriana told me, once again as if she were explaining something to a very young child. There was a touch of anxiety in her tone that might have said: 'You need watching. You could make a botch of this. You've got too much imagination. That's why I am here. Not everyone, you know, needs a cover.' But she didn't say that. What she said was: 'I've got a delivery to make. You can help if you like.'

She got out and went round to the doors of the van. The back was stacked with cases of apples and it was only now that I smelled them. We were parked in front of an open fruitshop that was also a bar, general store, phone-post and restaurant. Three or four tables without chairs stood in front of it, their white paint chipped with rust. I leaned into the van and took one of the boxes.

'No,' she told me, 'not that one. The one underneath. And be careful, it's heavier than you'd expect. I'll take the other one myself.'

We carried the two boxes through the empty shop into a passageway between the kitchen, which was deserted but clean, with all its metal surfaces polished, and two dirty lavatories, one of them without a door. A woman appeared from the rooms behind and Carla told her matter-of-factly: 'A delivery for Piero.' The woman nodded. 'No other message. Just the delivery and the fact that we called.' The woman, who was old, nodded again and drew a brown shawl around her shoulders. She was carrying a roll of grey knitting with enormous wooden needles plunged through the ball.

'Haven't you got time for coffee?'

'No,' Carla told her. 'We're not late but we haven't got time.'

The woman made a line with her lips. 'Good luck then.'

Carla stuck her hands deep into the pockets of her cardigan and lifted her chin in what I had always thought of as a haughty manner when she was a tall blond, but which now seemed merely nervous. It needed her darker appearance for me to see her as she really was. 'Come on,' she said, leading the way out.

She locked the back doors of the van, climbed in and we were soon speeding away again under the new spring leaves. 'If you want coffee,' she told me, 'there's a flask, and I brought sandwiches. I thought we'd stop and eat when we're further along the way.'

Two hours later, parked in a laneway off the main road, we ate ham rolls, drank a little white wine and had coffee. The rolls were wrapped in a linen tea-towel that was properly starched and ironed; there were paper napkins as well, paper cups for the wine and more for the coffee. But she had forgotten to bring sugar.

'Damn,' she said, 'damn, damn! How could I forget?' I had never seen her so disturbed. I thought of her admonishing God as she worked away with her rubber, eliminating errors, but the error this time was hers.

'Really, I don't mind at all,' I told her, sipping the bitter brew. 'I even prefer it.'

But my preferences, or my polite lies, were not the point. She had planned that everything down to the last detail should be right and her own forgetfulness upset her. It was more than a matter of bad housekeeping. It was as if some essential ingredient of the situation had been fatally overlooked, leaving a gap that could never be filled. If I could forget this, she seemed to say, I could forget anything. What is it that I have forgotten? She tried to taste what it was in the coffee, but it was not there.

When she started the car again it stalled. Another failure. She swore and seemed suddenly in a different mood. As if she had broken through out of one sort of weather into another, just as the day had with its lowering clouds and threat of rain. It occurred to me that to recover her earlier spirits she would have to push back the dark, close-fitting wig she wore and shake her blondness free. But of course it wasn't as simple as that. I recognized the thought as part of my own growing depression. The last station in our journey was past; there would be no more stops now before the final one. The little cabin, which four hours ago had been quite unfamiliar to me, had become a place I felt reluctant to leave. It was security. It was on the known side, the safe side of the event. And our meal together, which I had not thought about while we were eating it, was something I would gladly have gone back to savour: the crisp rolls, the whiteness of the tea-towel with its sharp creases, even the bitter coffee. They had, in retrospect, an importance, those shared moments of isolation together in the cabin, the food, the drink, that I ought to have lingered over, whereas I had simply accepted them and let them pass. 'Why,' I asked myself, 'do I understand things only when I am no longer part of them?' And that too depressed me. The change of weather in the cabin was all my own. That little business of the missing sugar might have affected Carla less than it affected me, and the wish that she would push back her wig and be Carla again was also for my sake, not hers. It would put us back in the safety of yesterday, or three hundred kilometres ago. I watched the numbers fall through the little window on the dashboard and was so mesmerized by them that I was hardly aware of the first drops of rain till we rode right into the storm, then out again into watery sunshine and shiny pavements, then into a longer stretch of it as we came to the outskirts of the town.

So I never did see what the place was like. We simply crawled along blind with our lights on, while headlamps and trees and misty soft-edged figures swarmed across the glass.

'We're almost there,' Carla Adriana said, peering over the curve of the wheel. 'I'll stop a moment under the arcades and we can have a cigarette. You'll hear the clock strike. Be sure to take everything with you.'

She was pushing her things, including the scraps of our picnic, into a leather shoulder-bag

'I'm to ditch the car in the parking lot in the next street. The car you are to look out for afterwards is a blue Renault with a local numberplate. It will be waiting at the corner, right beside the bank. The driver will take you to the edge of town and another car will take you on. Is all that clear?'

I nodded. She lit a cigarette and passed it to me, then lit another and threw her head back in the old way, drawing deep. We sat in silence.

I had expected in these last moments to have some power of control over myself; to close my eyes perhaps and count, or to think of one of those imaginary scenes that I had used as a child for putting myself to sleep and could still evoke on occasions, or even to find some formula of words, a poem, Ronsard's "Pour Hélène" which I had learned at highschool and which ever since had stayed irrelevantly in my head, or a prayer whose phrases could be repeated over and over till the time was filled. Instead I was invaded by blind panic and a hundred questions I wanted suddenly to put to Carla, not all of them by any means concerned with the matter in hand, and some of which she would be no more equipped to answer than I myself was. After all my weeks of preparation I was quite unready for what was to occur.

'Now.' she said. 'It's time.' She gave a quick glance at the rear vision mirror and started the motor. 'Go!'

I must have opened the door and stumbled out as I had earlier fallen asleep, simply on the authority of her voice, because almost instantly I was alone under the arcades, which were dripping after the storm. She was gone, and I was walking, with a dreamlike sense of everything having too sharp a focus, along the western edge of the piazza, past the unfrequented café and the shop that sells dress material and cushions.

The light was brilliantly clear, as it can be after a downpour and the square was full of pieces of sky with pigeons sipping at them or splashing up broken glass. A bell was tolling. People stood about with open umbrellas. Hot little raindrops were striking diagonally through the sunlight, and the façade opposite, which seemed un-nervingly close, too close for the square I had imagined, was luminous and golden, all its details hard-edged and precise as if newly carved.

It was like going back to a place of your childhood

and finding it familiar but wrong. All the dimensions were wrong. And I hadn't reckoned on the loudness of the bell or the shortness of the time it would take me to arrive at the platform, or, as the great central doors of the cathedral clanged and swung open, on the appearance right behind me of a uniformed beadle with a cocked hat and breeches, who stood for a moment before the open darkness where the doors had been with a wand held at arm's length before him and might have been about to knock three times for a performance to begin.

He stood, then lowered the wand in an exaggerated ceremonial fashion, and moved.

Behind him the priest and his acolytes in white linen. Behind them the coffin, on the shoulders of six uniformed ushers. Then at last the old man, looking so much more fragile than I had expected, a thin stooped figure with a skull like a baby's, almost transparent; you could see the blue veins in it, softly pulsing. He wore a morning coat and striped trousers and carried a shiny top hat. At his side the daughter, all in grey, had turned aside for a moment and was engaged in pushing up a black umbrella. As I stepped forward she glanced up. *An extraordinary woman*, I thought as our eyes met. Then she looked down and her mouth opened in what must have been a cry. She had seen the gun.

Time stopped for whole seconds as we stood there, simply staring at one another. She seemed tremendous, awful. I had a sudden sick impression of the full weight of what it was – flesh, bone, a spirit of female power and protection – that had taken up residence in the grey figure and was about to interpose itself between me and what I must do, and of the forty-nine years in which she had been gathering herself for it. Her shoulders rose, a thick wad of muscle appeared in her neck. She prepared to charge. At some point years before I was born this moment must have presented itself as what her whole life was making for. She saw that now and launched herself towards me, a creature out of another order of existence, fully armed, resplendent, and fixing me with a fierce gaze as if to say, *There, you thought this moment was yours and that you would control it, but look, it is mine.* She was the embodiment, in grey silk, of everything I had tried to exclude from the event and had known all along could not be excluded. How could that be? I had known it and only now saw what I knew.

A bullet struck her in the shoulder. She seemed unaware of it. It was when the second bullet tore into her that she fell back, staggered, and stood still, then began, very slowly, to sink to her knees; but with immense slowness, and with a look of infinite surprise and disappointment, as if drawn down by a natural force that she had tried with all her being to resist but which was, after all, too strong for her. She was only human. The angelic powers had deserted her. She still held on to the umbrella, like a parachute by which she would not be saved.

I stood over her with the unsteady Beretta. One of her hands flapped against the flagstones, which were greasy with blood, and the sounds that came from her open mouth might have been in another tongue. I leant forward a little to try and catch them. 'Bgrrr,' she thundered, 'Tgrrr, dgrrrr, mgrrrr.!' One part of me was held fascinated with the effort of trying to translate, and I thought that if I closed my eyes and listened in the dark the words might make sense and reveal their meaning to me. But another part of me had already turned away. There was still the old man.

He had straightened and turned at the woman's first cry of alarm and he stood halted now, staring right at me. It was the third and fourth shot that struck him, once in the breast, once in the throat, and he went down immediately. The remaining shots went off at random, entirely without my will, and I heard them resounding behind me as I broke away into the open square in the direction of the fourth of my seven photographs, all rinsed and new in the sunlight, and saw in my path as the noise rolled away behind me, Clara, blond again and with a coat over her arm that must have concealed the second weapon. My first thought was that she was about to shoot me. The bell went on tolling, and as I swerved away her image was replaced by that of the woman with the umbrella. She was kneeling right in my path, her hands raised, her mouth open, and the terrible sound that came out of it, the long agonized cry of an animal wounded beyond comprehension, was my own voice crying over and over words that I understood only too well. 'No! No! No!', like the tolling of a bell. Of the moment I had so carefully prepared for, the luminous moment when he and I would stand face to face in the full understanding of what was about to occur, I had no memory at all.

The blue Renault was there at the corner and in seconds I had reached it. The driver, a thin youth with a beard, was leaning across the front seat with his hand on the open door. 'For God's sake,' he hissed, 'get in. What are you waiting for?'

After long seconds in which everything had happened at a tenth of its normal pace, and every gesture seemed isolated, frozen, time was racing again and my heart with it. I sat slumped over the weapon, shaking so violently now that my teeth chattered. Some part of me was still stranded out there in the lurid square, utterly mesmerized before the kneeling figure of the woman, unable to move. It was a merely physical self that sat sweating in the promised Renault, making at high speed towards a set of traffic lights and very nearly safe on the other side of all this.

So that reality, when it impinged, seemed unreal.

'Oh no,' the driver moaned, swinging violently on to the kerb, 'it can't be! Jesus! Jes-*us*!'

There, immediately ahead, was a roadblock.

He flung open the door and tumbled out, leaving the engine running and the windscreen wipers flicking crazily back and forth, and through the waves of rain I saw lights flashing and uniformed men bearing down upon us. There were shots. At last my own door too was open, and as I stumbled out on to the pavement I thought *Yes, I have seen all this before in the newspapers. In black and white. In the odd, grainy dimension of what is already history.*

I was naked and in the open. Every landmark

beyond the piazza was unfamiliar to me, I was a stranger here and had lost all sense of direction. I hurled myself into an alleyway, hearing the shots die away behind, and felt what must have been the weight of my haversack fall away from me. *Good,* I thought. *So much the lighter. Now I have nothing.* I turned a corner, then another, and found myself in the piazza again – so I did see it a second time – facing the gothic palace with its blind brick loggia. The hearse for the disrupted funeral was there, a great black carriage all agleam in the rain, its glass windows banked with flowers, sable plumes at the corners, before it two coal-black horses solemnly decked and plumed. They lifted their heads as I passed and I caught a flash of white eyeballs. One of them raised a foreleg and struck the pavement, *clang, clang,* with its hoof. I cast myself into the street that curves away to the east of the palace, which had so fascinated me in the photographs and round whose bend in time I had been unable to see. There was no one in sight and no sound of pursuit.

The street with its overhanging eaves continued to curve, with heavy buildings on either side, all their shutters solemnly shut. I began to be breathless, and it occurred to me that with my footsteps echoing as they did between the high walls I might attract less attention if I simply walked.

So I walk.

Out here in the big open square I have come to there has been no rain, not a sign of it. I cross the square, which is deserted, and which seems enormous at the pace I am forcing myself to adopt, turn down a narrow side street and am a little surprised to discover that I am already at the edge of town. There are derelict sheds standing among waist-high thistles, broken fences grown over with old man's beard, stretches of stony ground scattered with rags, paper, plastic bottles, worn car tyres, tennis shoes, rusty food-tins, the gathered wrack and rubbish of existence, and a yard beside a disused cinema where boys have been tinkering with a car. All the parts of it are laid out neatly in the dirt. A blue Renault.

A little further on and I find orchards on both sides of the road, apple trees lit up with late afternoon sunlight and heavy with fruit. I reach up and take one. Bite into it. Eat.

And in the miraculous assurance of being safe at last, walk on under the early blossoms.

THE BREAD OF TIME TO COME

For Elizabeth Riddell

Man is an exception, whatever else he is. If it is not true that a divine creature fell, then we can only say that one of the animals went entirely off its head.

G.K. Chesterton

Here is the bread of time to come,

Here is the actual stone. The bread
Will be out bread, the stone will be

Our bed and we shall sleep by night.
We shall forget by day, except

The moment when we choose to play
The imagined pine, the imagined jay.

Wallace Stevens

1

All morning, far over to his left where the light of the swamp ended and farmlands began, a clumsy shape had been lifting itself out of an invisible paddock and making slow circuits of the air, climbing, dipping, rolling a little, then disappearing below the trees.

The land in that direction rose gradually towards far, intensely blue mountains that were soft blue at this time of day but would later approach purple. The swamp was bordered with tea-trees, some of them half-standing in water and staining the shallows there a tobacco brown. Its light was dulled by cloud shadows, then, as if an unseen hand were rubbing it with a cloth, it brightened, flared, and the silver shone through.

A vast population of waterbirds lived in the swamp, and in the paddocks and wooded country beyond were lorikeets, rosellas and the different families of pigeons – fruit-pigeon, bronze-wings, the occasional topknot or squatter – and high over all stood the birds of prey, the hawks and kestrels. But the big shadow was that of a bi-plane that all morning rose and dipped, its canvas drawn tight across struts, all its piano-wires singing. It was a new presence here and it made Jim Saddler uneasy. He watched it out of the corner of his eye and resented its bulk, the lack of purpose in its appearance and disappearance at the tree line, the lack of pattern in its lumbering passes, and the noise it made, which was also a disturbance and new.

Over behind him, where all this swampland drained into the Pacific, were dunes, shifting sand held together with purple-flowering pigweed and silvery scrub; then the surf – miles of it. You could walk for hours beside its hissing white and never see a soul. Just great flocks of gulls, and pied oyster-catchers flitting over the wet light, stopping, starting off again; not at random but after tiny almost transparent crabs, and leaving sharp, three-toed prints.

He had a map of all this clearly in his head, as if in every moment of lying here flat on his belly watching some patch of it for a change of shape or colour that would be a small body betraying itself, he were also seeing it from high up, like the hawk, or that fellow in his flying-machine. He moved always on these two levels, through these two worlds: the flat world of individual grassblades, seen so close up that they blurred, where the ground-feeders darted about striking at worms, and the long view in which all this part of the country was laid out like a relief-map in the Shire Office – surf, beach, swampland, wet paddocks, dry, forested hill-slopes, jagged blue peaks. Each section of it supported its own birdlife; the territorial borders of each kind were laid out there, invisible but clear, which the birds were free to cross but didn't; they stayed for the most part within strict limits. They stayed. Then at last, when the time came, they upped and left; flew off in groups, or in couples or alone, to where they came from and lived in the other part of the year, far out over the earth's rim in the Islands, or in China or Europe.

Holding one of them in the glasses he was aware of that also. *This creature that I could catch so easily in my hands, feeling the heart beat and the strong wings flutter against my palms, has been further and higher even than that clumsy plane. It has been to Siberia. Its tiny quick eye has seen something big. A whole half of the earth.*

The bi-plane appeared again, climbing steeply against the sun. Birds scattered and flew up in all directions. It flopped down among them, so big, so awkward, so noisy. Did they wonder what it ate? A hundred times bigger than any hawk or eagle its appetite would be monstrous. Did they keep their sharp eyes upon it?

Jim's eye was on the swamphen. He had been watching it for nearly an hour with a pair of field-glasses provided by Ashley Crowther. There was a nest on a platform there among the reeds, with maybe five or six creamy-brown eggs.

Ashley Crowther was a young man, not all that much older than himself, who had been away to school in England and then at Cambridge, and had recently come back to manage his father's land. He owned all the land beyond the swamp and from the swamp towards the ocean. The bi-plane was flying out of one of Ashley Crowther's paddocks and was piloted, Jim guessed, by one of Ashley's friends. There were regular weekend-guests at the homestead these days, young fellows, and also ladies, who arrived in automobiles wearing caps or with their heads swathed in voile against the dust of country roads, to ride, to eat big meals in the lamplit house and to dance to gramophone music on the verandah.

The swampland also belonged to Ashley, and because he was interested in the birds he had set Jim to watch it and to record its various comings and goings. It was a new idea that came from Europe, though Queensland in fact had passed a law to protect birds nearly forty years ago, before any other place in the Empire.

Ashley Crowther had sat on a log chewing a grass-stem and looked out dreamily over the swamp, and Jim had recognized right off a man he could talk to, even if they said nothing at all; and had shifted his feet, unused to this, and uncertain where it might lead. It wasn't his place to make an opening.

'Listen,' Ashley had said. With no preliminaries, as if the whole thing had just that moment taken shape in his head, he laid out his plan; and Jim, who till then had been merely drifting, and might have drifted as far as the city and become a mill-hand or a tram-conductor, saw immediately the scope of it and felt his whole life change. A moment before this odd bloke had been a stranger. Now he stuck out his hand to be shaken and there was all the light of the swampland

and its swarming life between them, of which Jim was to have sole charge.

He was twenty, and Ashley Crowther was a tall, inarticulate young man of twenty-three, who looked at times as if he was stooping under the weight of his watch-chain and who stumbled not only over words but over his own boots. But he had said 'Well then, you're my man,' having that sort of power, and Jim was made. All the possibilities that for the past two years had tugged and nagged at him – the city, marriage, drink, the prospect of another thirty years of dragging his boot over sawdust in the Anglers' Arms, of sitting reading the sports page with his feet propped on the bed-head while rain dripped into a basin on his bedroom floor, the sullenness and hard-jawed resentment of months that were all Sundays – suddenly hauled off and lifted. He was made free of his own life.

'Jim's a new man,' his father told his drinking mates up at the pub with studied gloom. He had projected for Jim a life as flat, save for the occasional down-turn, as his own. It was inevitable, he declared, 'for the likes of us.'

'What does it mean,' Jim had wanted to ask, 'the likes of us?' Except for the accidental link of blood he saw nothing in common between his father and himself and resented the cowardly acceptance of defeat that made his father feel this change in his fortunes as a personal affront. But he had had enough cuffs from the old man, over lesser issues than this, to have learned that there were some questions that were better not put.

'You're a bloody fool,' the old man told him, 'if you trust that lot, with their fancy accents and their new-fangled ideas. And their machines! You'd be better off gettin' a job in Brisbane and be done with it. Better off, y'hear? Better!' And he punched hard into the palm of his hand.

There was in his father a kind of savagery that Jim kept at arm's length; not because he feared to be its victim in the physical sense – he had been often enough and it was nothing much, it was merely physical – but because he didn't want to be infected. It was of a kind that could blast the world. It allowed nothing to exist under its breath without being blackened, torn up by the roots, slashed at, and shown when ripped apart to have a centre as rotten as itself. His father had had a hard life, but that didn't explain it. 'I was sent out to work at ten years old by *my* old man. Put to the plough like a bloody animal. Sent to sleep in straw. All that, all that!' But it didn't account for what the man was. It had happened equally to others in those days; and besides, Jim might have argued, did you treat me any better? No, the baleful look his father turned on the world had no reason, it simply was.

He swallowed his resentment and determined to say no more. As for Ashley Crowther, he would take the risk. Something in the silence that existed between them, when they just sat about on stumps and Ashley crossed his legs and rested his chin in the palm of his hand, made Jim believe there could be common ground between them, whatever the difference. There was in Ashley a quiet respect for things that Jim also respected.

None of this had to be stated. Ashley was too incoherent to have explained and Jim would have been embarrassed to hear it, but he understood. All this water, all these boughs and leaves and little clumps of tussocky grass that were such good nesting-places and feeding grounds belonged inviolably to the birds. The rights that could be granted to a man by the Crown, either for ninety-nine years or in perpetuity, were of another order and didn't quite mean what they said. This strange man with his waistcoat and his watch-chain, his spotted silk tie and Pommie accent, had seen that from the start.

But there was more. There was also, on Ashley's part, a recognition that Jim too had rights here, that these acres might also belong, though in another manner, to him. Such claims were ancient and deep. They lay in Jim's knowledge of every blade of grass and drop of water in the swamp, of every bird's foot that was set down there; in his having a vision of the place and the power to give that vision breath; in his having, most of all, the names for things and in that way possessing them. It went beyond mere convention or the law.

There was something here, Jim thought, that answered his unasked question, 'what does it mean, the likes of us?', by cancelling it out in some larger view, and it was this that he was prepared to trust. The view was Ashley's and it was generous. It made a place for Jim, and left room as well for the coming and going of a thousand varieties, even the most alien, of birds.

2

Ashley Crowther had come home after more than twelve years to find himself less a stranger here than he expected.

He had been at school in England, then at Cambridge, then in Germany for a year studying music, and might have passed anywhere on that side of the world for an English gentleman. He spoke like one; he wore the clothes – he was much addicted to waistcoats and watch-chains, an affectation he might have to give up, he saw, in the new climate; he knew how to handle waiters, porters, commissionaires etc. with just the right mixture of authority, condescension and jolly good humour. He was in all ways cultivated, and his idleness, which is what people here would call it, gave him no qualms. He took a keen interest in social questions, and saw pretty clearly that in the coming years there would be much to be done, stands to be taken, forces to be resisted, changes to be made and come to terms with. The idea excited him. He approved of change. With all that to think of he didn't see that one had also to have a vocation, a job named and paid for and endured for a certain number of hours each day, to be a serious person.

Ashley Crowther was a very serious person. He was dreamy, certainly, and excitably inarticulate, but he liked what was practical, what worked, and in the three years since he came of age had owned four automobiles. Now he was interested in the newest thing of all, the air. He didn't fly himself, but his friend Bert did, and he was quite content, as in other cases, to play the patron and look on.

In the crude categories that had been in operation at Cambridge, athlete or aesthete, he had found himself willy-nilly among the latter. He had never been much good at games – his extreme thinness was against him – and he not only played the piano, Chopin and Brahms, but could whistle all the *Leitmotifs* from *The Ring*. But his childhood had been spent in the open, he had never lost his pleasure in wide spaces and distant horizons, in climbing, riding, going on picnics, and the creatures he had been surrounded by in those early years had never deserted his dreams. Moving as they did in the other half of the world, far under the actualities of the daylight one, they had retained their primitive power and kept him in touch with a continent he had been sent away from at eleven but never quite left. Perhaps that is why when he came back at twenty-three he was not a stranger.

Waking up that first morning in the old house – not in his own room, the room of his childhood, but in the big main bedroom since he was now the master – he had been overwhelmed by the familiarity of things:

the touch of the air on his skin – too warm; the sharpness of the light even at twenty to seven – it might have been noon elsewhere; above all, since it is what came closest to the centre of his being, the great all-embracing sound that rose from the dazzling earth, a layered music, dense but deeply flowing, that was clippered insects rubbing their legs together, bird-notes, grass-stems chaffing and fretting in the breeze. It immediately took him up and carried him back. He stepped out on to the verandah in his pyjamas – no need for even the lightest gown – and it was all about him, the whole scene trembled upon it. The flat earth had been transposed into another form and made accessible to a different sense. An expansive monotone, its excited fluting and throbbing and booming from distended throats had been the ground-bass, he saw, of every music he had ever known. It was the sound his whole being moved to. He stood barefoot on the gritty boards and let it fill his ear.

'How can you do it?' his friends back there had said, commiserating but admiring his courage, which they altogether exaggerated.

'It's my fate,' he had replied.

The phrase pleased him. It sounded solemn and final. But he was glad just the same to discover, now he was here, that he was not a stranger, and to feel, looking out on all this, the contentment of ownership and continuity.

It was his grandfather who had taken up the claim and put his name to the deeds; but he had died while the land was still wild in his head, a notion, no more, of what he had staked out in a strange and foreign continent that his children must make real. Ashley's father had created most of what lay before him. Now it was his.

There was still everything to do – one saw that at a glance. But Ashley saw things differently from his father and grandfather. They had always had in mind a picture they had brought from 'home', orderly fields divided by hedgerows, to which the present landscape, by planning and shaping, might one day be made to approximate. But for Ashley this was the first landscape he had known and he did not impose that other, greener one upon it; it was itself. Coming back, he found he liked its mixture of powdery blues and greens, its ragged edges, its sprawl, the sense it gave of being unfinished and of offering no prospect of being finished. These things spoke of space, and of a time in which nature might be left to go its own way and still yield up what it had to yield; there was that sort of abundance. For all his cultivation, he liked what was unmade here and could, without harm, be left that way.

There was more to Ashley Crowther's image of the world than his formal clothes might have suggested – though he was, in fact, without them at this moment, barefoot on scrubbed boards – or, since he was shy, his formal manners, which were not so easily laid aside.

After breakfast he changed into a cotton shirt, twills, boots and wide-brimmed hat and took a ride round his property, beginning with the little iron fenced enclosure where his parents, his grandparents and several smaller brothers and sisters were interred under sculptured stone.

The Monuments, as they were called, were only visible from the house when the big wheat-paddock was bare, since they stood in the very middle of it. He remembered how, as a child, he had crawled in among the rustling stems to find the place, his lost ancestral city, or had sat on a fence-post while a harvester, moving in wide circles, had gradually revealed it: tall columns standing alone among the flattened grain, already, even in those days, so chipped and stained that they might have been real monuments going back centuries rather than a mere score of years to the first death. He made his way towards them now, through the standing wheat, and sat for a moment with his hat off. Then rode on.

He saw much that day, though nothing like the whole – that would take weeks, months even. In the evening, after bathing and changing, he sat alone on the verandah and decided he would make the house, once again, a place where people came; he couldn't keep all this, or his excitement in it, to himself. The smokiness of the hour, the deepening blue of the hills and all the gathering night sounds, were too good not to share, and he was by nature generous.

Within two months he had done all that. He had visited most places on the property and got a clear view of all its various activities and the men who were in charge or carried them out. When he looked at the manager's books now he saw real faces behind the names, and behind the figures fenced places and wild, and knew what it all meant in hours worked and distance covered. It had found its way down, painfully at first, then pleasurably, into his wiry muscles, in days of riding or walking or sitting about yarning in the sun.

The house too had been given a new life. Weekend guests came and were put up in the big verandah rooms with their cedar wardrobes and tiled wash-stands and basins. They strolled on the verandah in the early morning, having been drawn out by the brightness of the light, and sat in deep squatters' chairs in the evening to enjoy the dusk, while Ashley, supplementing the music of the landscape itself, played to them on an upright. They ate huge meals under a fan in the dining-room, with a lazy Susan to deal at breakfast with four different sorts of jam and two of honey, one a comb, and at dinner with the sauces and condiments; they took picnics down to the creek. The tennis court was weeded and spread with a reddish-pink hard stuff that was made from smashed anthills, and they played doubles, the ladies in skirts and blouses, the young men in their shirtsleeves. Bert came with his flying-machine. They watched it wobble in over the swamp, then circle the house and touch down, a bit unsteadily, in the home paddock. It sat there in the heat haze like a giant bird or moth while cows flicked their tails among cow-pats, and did not seem out of place. It was a landscape, Ashley thought, that could accommodate a good deal. That was his view of it. It wasn't so clearly defined as England or Germany; new things could enter and find a place there. It might be old, even very old, but it was more open than Europe to what was still to come.

He also discovered Jim.

While he was riding one day in the low scrub along the swamp the young man had simply started up out of the earth at his feet; or rather, had rolled over on his back, where he had been lying in the grass, and then got to his feet cursing. Ashley hadn't seen the other creature that started up yards off and went flapping into a tree. He was too astonished that some fellow should be lying there on his belly in the middle of nowhere, right under the horse's hooves, and felt the oath, though he didn't necessarily attach it to himself, to be on the whole unjustified.

The young man stood, thin-faced, heavy shouldered, in worn moleskins and a collarless shirt, and made no attempt to explain his presence or to acknowledge any difference between Ashley and himself except that one was mounted and the other had his two feet set firmly on the earth. He brushed grass-seed from his trousers with an old hat and stood his ground. Ashley, oddly, found this less offensive than he ought.

'What were you doing?' he asked. It was a frank curiosity he expressed. There was nothing of reproach in it.

'Watchin' that Dollar bird,' Jim told him. 'You scared it off.'

'Dollar bird?'

'Oriental,' Jim said. 'Come down from the Moluccas.'

His voice was husky and the accent broad; he drawled. The facts he gave were unnecessary and might have been pedantic. But when he named the bird, and again when he named the island, he made them sound, Ashley thought, extraordinary. He endowed them with some romantic quality that was really in himself. An odd interest revealed itself, the fire of an individual passion.

Ashley slipped down from the saddle and they stood side by side, the grass almost at thigh level. Jim pointed.

'It's in that ironbark, see?' He screwed up his eyes. 'There, over to the left. Second branch from the top. Red beak. Purple on the throat and tail-feathers. See?'

Ashley stared, focused, found the branch; and then, with a little leap of surprise and excitement, the bird – red beak, purple throat, all as the young man had promised.

'I can see it!' he exclaimed, just like a child, and they both grinned. The young man turned away and sat on a log. He took the makings of a smoke from his pocket. Ashley stumbled forward.

'Have one of mine,' he insisted. 'No, really.' He offered the case, already snapped open, with the gold-tipped tailor-mades under a metal band that worked like a concertina.

'Thanks,' the young man said, his square fingers making an awkward job of working the band. He turned the cylinder, so utterly smooth and symmetrical, in his fingers, looking at the gold paper round the tip, then put it to his lower lip, struck a wax match, which he cupped in his hand against the breeze, and held it out to Ashley, who dipped his head towards it and blew out smoke. Jim lit his own cigarette and flipped the match with his thumbnail. All this action carried them over a moment of nothing-more-to-say into an easy silence. Ashley led his horse to a stump opposite, and crossing his legs, and with his body hunched forward elbow to knee, fell intensely still, then said abruptly:

'Are you out here often? Watching, I mean?'

'Fairly.'

'Why?'

'I dunno. It's something to do, isn' it?' He looked about, his grey eyes narrowed, and the land was a flat circle all round, grass-tips, tree-stumps, brush, all of it seemingly still and silent, all of it crowded and alive with eyes, beaks, wing-tips.

Ashley followed his gaze. The land shifted into a clearer focus, and he might himself have been able, suddenly, to see it in all its detail, the individual eye infinitesimally rolling, the red beak in a spray of gum-flowers, the tiny body at ground level among the roots, one of the seed-eaters, coloured like the earth. He was intensely aware for a moment how much life there might be in any square yard of it. And he owned a thousand acres.

But even if he looked and saw, he would have no name for it. *Dollar bird*. This youth had the names.

'Where did you learn?' he asked, out of where his own thoughts had led him.

'Oh, here 'n there. Some of it from books. Mostly,

you know, it's –' Jim found it difficult to explain that it was almost a sense he had, inexplicable even to himself. To have said that might have been to claim too much. A gift. Was it a gift? 'In time,' he said, 'you get to know some things and the rest you guess. If you're any good you guess right. Nine times in a hundred,' and he gave a laugh. Ashley laughed too. He drew himself tighter together, the knotted legs, the elbows in hard against his body, and the laughter was like an imp he had bottled up in there that suddenly came bubbling out.

'Listen,' he said, 'how would you like to work for me? How would you –'

He stopped, breathless with the excitement of it. The landscape, the whole great circle of it, grass-heads, scrub, water, sky, quite took his breath away. All those millions of lives as they entering what he had just conceived. 'How would you like,' he said, 'to do all this on a proper basis? I mean, make lists. We could turn this' (it was the notion of time that took his breath away, the years, the decades), 'into an observing place, a sanctuary. It's mine, I can make what I want of it. And you'd be just the man.'

Smoke trailed from Jim's lips in a steady stream. He had been waiting for so long for something like this to present itself, and now this Ashley Crowther fellow comes up behind him on a horse and offers it, just like that – not just a job but work, years, a lifetime.

The young man's silence threw Ashley off balance.

'I'd make it worth your while, of course.' He swallowed. The landscape itself, he thought, ought to add its appeal; for it was an appeal more than an offer he was making, and it was on the land's behalf that it was made. 'How does it strike you, then?' he asked lamely.

Jim nodded. 'It sounds alright.'

'Well then,' Ashley said, laughing and jumping to his feet, 'you're my man.' He thrust his hand out, and both standing now, feet on the ground, at the centre, if they could have seen themselves, of a vast circle of grass and low greyish scrub, with beyond them on one side tea-trees then paddocks, and on the other tea-trees then swamp then surf, in a very formal manner, with Ashley stooping slightly since he was so much the taller, and Jim quite square, they shook on it. It was done.

3

If Ashley discovered Jim, it was Jim who discovered Miss Harcourt, Miss Imogen Harcourt.

He was on his belly again, with a note-pad in his pocket, a stub of pencil behind his ear and the field-glasses Ashley Crowther had provided screwed firmly into his head – they might have been a fixture.

He was watching a sandpiper in a patch of marshy bank, one of the little wood sandpipers that appear each summer and come, most of them, from Northern Asia or Scandanavia, nesting away at the top of the world on the tundras or in the Norwegian snows and making their long way south.

It amazed him, this. That he could be watching, on a warm day in November, with the sun scorching his back, the earth pricking below and the whole landscape dazzling and shrilling, a creature that only weeks ago had been on the other side of the earth and had found its way here across all the cities of Asia, across lakes, deserts, valleys between high mountain ranges, across oceans without a single guiding mark, to light on just this bank and enter the round frame of his binoculars; completely contained there in its small life – striped breast and sides, white belly, yellow legs, the long beak investigating a pool for food, occasionally lifting its head to make that peculiar three-note whistle – and completely containing, somewhere invisibly within, that blank white world of the northern ice-cap and the knowledge, laid down deep in the tiny brain, of the air-routes and courses that had brought it here. Did it know where it had arrived on the earth's surface? Did it retain, in that small eye, some image of the larger world, so that it could say *There I was so many darknesses ago and now I am here, and will stay a time, and then go back*; seeing clearly the space between the two points, and knowing that the distance, however great, could quite certainly be covered a second time in the opposite direction because the further side was still visible, either there in its head or in the long memory of its kind.

The idea made Jim dizzy. That, or the sun, or the effort of watching. He raised the glasses to rest a moment, and in doing so caught something unexpected that flashed through the frames and was gone.

Where?

He let the glasses travel across, back, up a little, down, making various frames for the landscape, and there it was again: a face under a sun-bonnet. It was lined and brown, and was at the moment intensely fixed upon something, utterly absorbed. He shifted the glasses and found a black box on a tripod. The face ducked down behind it. The composite figure that now filled the frame was of a grey skirt, voluminous and rather bedraggled, topped by the black box wearing a sun-bonnet. The black box was pointing directly towards him. Could it be him that she was photographing?

It was only after a minute that he realized the truth. What the woman had in her sights was the same sandpiper he had been holding, just a few seconds ago, in his binoculars. For some time, without either of them being aware of it, they had, in all this landscape, and among all its creatures, been fixing their attention from different sides on the same spot and on the same small white-breasted body.

He wasn't all that much surprised by the coincidence. It seemed less extraordinary than that this few ounces of feather and bone should have found its way here from Siberia or Norway. That was itself so unlikely that men had preferred to believe, and not so long ago, either, that when the season turned, some birds had simply changed their form as others changed their plumage – that swallows, for example, became toads – and had actually given detailed accounts of the transformation: the birds gathering in such numbers, on reeds, on lake beds, that the stems bent low under their weight, and at the point where the reeds touched the water the swallows were transmuted, drew in their wings and heads, splayed their beaks to a toad-mouth, lowered their shrill cries to a throaty creaking, and went under the surface till it was time for them to be re-born overnight in their old shapes in twittering millions.

Meanwhile the tripod had transformed itself back

into a woman. She was stomping about in her grey skirt; an old girl, he guessed, of more than fifty, with grey curls under the bonnet and boots under the skirt. She lifted the tripod, snapped it shut, set it over her shoulder, and moved off with the rest of her equipment into the scrub.

Later, at the Anglers' Arms, he discovered her name and went down river to the weatherboard cottage she had bought and introduced himself.

The house was in bad shape. Sheets of iron were lifting from the roof, making the whole thing look as if it had grown wings and were about to rise out of this patch of scrub and settle in another on the far side of the hill. The weatherboard was grey, there were gaps in the verandah rails, and one window that had lost its glass was stuffed with yellowish newspaper. Stumps of what might once have been a paling fence stuck up here and there in a wilderness of briars, and beyond them, in the yard, a lemon tree had gone back to the wild state, with big lumpy fruit among inch-long thorns. On one side of the concrete step to the verandah was a washing tub, all pitted and crumbling with rust. It contained a skeletal fern. On the other two kerosene tins packed with dry earth put forth miraculous carnations, pink and white.

'Anyone home?' he called.

There was a voice from somewhere within, but so far off that it seemed to be replying from the depths of a house several times larger than this one, a deep hallway leading to cool, richly furnished rooms.

'Who is it?' An English voice.

'Me,' he replied foolishly, as a child would; then added in a deeper voice, 'Jim Saddler. I work for Mr Crowther.'

'Come on in,' the voice invited, 'I'll be with you in just a moment. I'm in the dark room.'

He stepped across a broken board, pushed the door and went in. It was clean enough, the kitchen, but bare: a scrubbed table and one chair, cups on hooks, a wood stove in a corrugated iron alcove. Wood-chunks, newspapers, a coloured calender.

'I can't come for a bit,' the voice called. 'Take a seat.'

The voice, he thought, might not have belonged to the woman he had seen out there in the swamp. It sounded younger, like that of someone who keeps up a running conversation while sitting in close conference with a chip-heater and six inches of soapy water; the voice of a woman engaged on something private, intimate, who lets you just close enough, with talk, to feel uncomfortable about what you cannot see. He didn't have much idea what happened in dark-rooms; photography was a mystery.

He examined the calendar. Pictures of English countryside. Turning the leaves back to January, then forward again through the year. Minutes passed.

'There!' she said, and came out pinning a little gold watch to the tucked bodice of her blouse. She was a big, round-faced woman, and the grey curls now that he saw them without the bonnet looked woollen, they might have been a wig.

'Jim Saddler,' he said again, rising.

She offered her hand, which was still damp where

she had just dried it, and they shook. Her handshake, he thought, was firmer than his. At least, it was to begin with.

'Imogen Harcourt. Would you like tea?'

'Thanks,' he said, 'if it's no trouble.'

He wondered about the one chair.

'I've come about that sandpiper,' he said straight out. 'I seen you taking a picture of it.'

'Did you?'

'Yes I did. I work for Ashley Crowther, *Mister* Crowther, I'm his bird man. I keep lists –.' He was shy of making too much of it and made too little. He could never bring himself to say the word that might have properly explained.

'I know,' she admitted, swinging back to face him with the filled kettle in her hand. 'I've seen you. I saw you yesterday.'

'Did you?' he said foolishly, not being used to that; to being *seen*. 'Well then,' he said, 'we're more or less on terms.'

She laughed. 'More or less. Do you take milk?'

She couldn't tell for the moment whether they would be friends or not; whether he had come here to share something or to protect a right. He was awkward, he had dignities. His pale hair stuck out straw-like where it was unevenly but closely cropped, and he stood too much at attention, as if defending narrow ground.

Jim too was puzzled. It was mostly younger women who spoke straight up at you like that, out of the centre of their own lives. Pretty women. Wives, mothers, unmarried aunts had generally settled more comfortably into the conventions than Miss Imogen Harcourt had; they tried harder to please. Though she wasn't what his father would have called a character. She was independent but not odd.

They drank their tea. There was, after all, no trouble about the chair. She half-sat, half-leaned on the window-ledge, and told him at once, without prompting, what there was to tell of her story. She had come here from Norfolk, six years ago, with a brother who'd had a mind to try gold-mining and gone to Mount Morgan but had failed to make a fortune and gone home again. She had decided to stay. She offered no explanation of that. What her intention had been in first following her brother to the other side of the world and then failing to follow him home again was not revealed. She had a small income and was supplementing it by taking nature photographs for a London magazine.

'Birds,' Jim specified.

'Not always. But yes, often enough. That sandpiper took my fancy because it was one of my favourites at home – they come down from the north, you know, and winter among us. In Norfolk, I mean.'

'And here.'

'Yes, here too. It's odd, isn't it? To come halfway across the world and find –. It made me feel homesick. So I set up quickly, got a good shot, and there it is. Homesickness dealt with. Stuffed into the box.'

He found he understood almost everything she said straight off, and this was unusual.

'Could I see it? The photo?'

'Why not?'

She led him into the hallway, past what must have been a bedroom, and into the darkness at the end of the hall.

It was the best room in the house; orderly, well set-up, with two sinks, a lamp, black cloth to cover the windows. He understood that too. When he stepped into the place it wasn't just the narrowness of the space they stood in, among all the apparatus of a hobby, or trade, that made him feel they had moved closer. He saw, because she allowed him to see, a whole stretch of her life, wider, even here in a dark-room, than anything he could have guessed from what she had already told – Norfolk, her brother, the tent city at Mount Morgan. He liked the order, the professionalism, the grasp all this special equipment suggested of a competence. There were racks for her plates, bottles of chemicals all neatly labelled, rubber gloves, a smell of something more than lavender.

'So this is it,' he said admiringly as he might have spoken to any man. 'Where you work.'

'Yes,' she said, 'here and out there.'

As he was to discover, she often made these distinctions, putting things clearer, moving them into a sharper focus.

'The light, and then the dark.'

She took a sheet of paper and offered it to him, and looked anxious as he subjected it to scrutiny.

It was the sandpiper. Perfect. Every speckle, every stripe on the side where it faded off into the white of the underbelly, the keen eye in the lifted head – he felt oddly moved to see the same bird in this other dimension. Moved too at the trouble it must have taken, and the quick choices, to get just that stance, which was so perfectly characteristic; her own keen eye measuring the bird's and discovering the creature's taut, spring-like alertness. Did she know so much about birds? Or did some intuition guide her? *This is it; this is the moment when we see into the creature's unique life*. That too might be a gift.

The sandpiper was in sharp focus against a blur of earth and grass-stems, as if two sets of binoculars had been brought to bear on the same spot, and he knew that if the second pair could now be shifted so that the landscape came up as clear as the bird, he too might be visible, lying there with a pair of glasses screwed into his head. He was there but invisible; only he and Miss Harcourt might ever know that he too had been in the frame, hidden among those soft rods of light that were grass-stems and the softer sunbursts that were grass-heads or tiny flowers. To the unenlightened eye there was just the central image of the sandpiper with its head attentively cocked. And that was as it should be. It was the sandpiper's picture.

'Perfect,' he breathed.

'Yes,' she said, 'I was pleased too.'

They looked at the bird between them, having moved quickly, since yesterday, to where they now stood with just this sheet of paper between them on which the bird's passage through its own brief huddle of heat and energy had been caught for a moment and fixed, maybe for ever.

'I must show this,' Jim said, 'to Ashley Crowther.'

So they became partners, all three, and a week later Jim told her of the sanctuary, actually using the word out loud for the first time, since he was certain now that there was nothing in her that would scoff at the grandness of it, but blushing just the same; the blood rose right up into the lobes of his ears.

He never uttered the word again. He didn't have to. When he talked to Miss Harcourt, as when he talked to Ashley Crowther, they spoke only of 'the birds'.

4

Sometimes, when Ashley Crowther had a party of friends down for the weekend, or for the Beaudesert races, Jim would take them out in a flat-bottomed boat, and for an hour or two they would drift between dead white trees over brackish water, its depths the colour of brewed tea, its surface a layer of drowned pollen inches thick in places, a burnished gold. Parting the scum, they would break in among clouds.

Ashley would be in the bow, his knees drawn up hard under his chin, his arms, in shirt-sleeves, propped upon them, like some sort of effigy, Jim thought – an image of whatever god it was that had charge of this place, a waterbird transmuted. The women, and the young men in blazers who shared the centre of the boat with their provisions, a wicker basket, its silver hasp engraved with the name of the house, would be subdued, tense, held on a breath; held on Jim's breath.

'That,' he would whisper, lifting the pole and letting them slide forward in the stillness, 'is the Sacred Kingfisher. From Borneo.'

The name, in Jim's hushed annunciation of it,

immediately wrapped the bird in mystery, beyond even the brilliance of its colouring and the strange light the place touched it with.

'And over there – see? – those are lotus birds. See? Far over. Aw, now they've seen us, they're off. They've got a nest at the edge there, right down at water level. See their feet? Long they are. That's for walking on the lotus leaves, or on waterlily pads, so they don't sink.'

He would push his pole into mud again, putting his shoulder into it and watching the birds flock away, and they would ride smoothly in under the boughs. Nobody spoke. It was odd the way the place imposed itself and held them. Even Ashley Crowther, who preferred music, was silent here and didn't fidget. He sat spell-bound. *And maybe*, Jim thought, *this is music too, this sort of silence*.

What he could not know was to how great a degree these trips into the swamp, in something very like a punt, were for Ashley recreations of long, still afternoons on the Cam, but translated here not only to another hemisphere, but back, far back, into some pre-classical, pre-historic, primaeval and haunted world (it was this that accounted for his mood of suspended wonder) in which the birds Jim pointed out, and might almost have been calling up as he named them in a whisper out of the mists before creation, were extravagantly disguised spirits of another order of existence, and the trip itself – despite the picnic hamper and the champagne bottles laid in ice, and the girls, one of whom was the girl he was about to marry – a water journey in another, deeper sense; which is why he occasionally shivered, and might, looking back, have seen Jim, where he leaned on the pole, straining, a slight crease in his brow and his teeth biting into his lower lip, as the ordinary embodiment of a figure already glimpsed in childhood and given a name in mythology, and only now made real.

'There,' Jim breathed, 'white ibis. They're common enough really. Beautiful, but.' He lifted his eyes in admiration, and at the end of the sentence, his voice as well, to follow their slow flight as they beat away. They might have been swimming, stroke on stroke, through the heavy air. 'And that's a stilt, see? See its blue back? It's a real beauty!'

They would be stilled in the boat, all wonder, who at other times were inclined to giggle, the girls, and worry about their hair or the sit of their clothes, and the young men to stretch their legs and yawn. They were so graceful, these creatures, turning their slow heads as the boat glided past and doubled where the water was clear: marsh terns, spotted crake, spur-winged plover, Lewin water rails. And Jim's voice also held them with its low excitement. He was awkward and rough-looking till they got into the boat. Then he too was light, delicately balanced, and when it was a question of the birds, he could be poetic. They looked at him in a new light and with a respect he wouldn't otherwise have been able to command.

As for Ashley, he liked to show them off: his birds. Or rather, he liked to have Jim show them off, and was pleased at dinner afterwards when his guests praised the ibis, the Sacred Kingfisher, the water rail, as if he had been very clever indeed in deciding that this is what he should collect rather than Meissen figures or Oriental mats.

But in the boat, in the place where the creatures were at home, they passed out of his possession as strangely as they had passed into it, and he might have been afraid then of his temerity in making a claim; they moved with their little lives, if they moved at all, so transiently across his lands – even when they were natives and spent their whole lives there – and knew nothing of Ashley Crowther. They shocked him each time he came here with the otherness of their being. He could never quite accept that they were, he and these creatures, of the same world. It was as if he had inherited a piece of the next world, or some previous one. That was why he felt such awe when Jim so confidently offered himself as an intermediary and named them: 'Look, the Sacred Kingfisher. From Borneo.'

When they stopped to picnic there was talk at last. They came back to reality.

'The nightingale,' a Mrs McNamara informed them, 'that's the most beautiful of all songbirds now.'

'I've never heard it,' a younger woman regretted.

'Oh it's beautiful,' Mrs McNamara assured her. 'But you have to go to Europe. Alas, my love, it was the nightingale.'

'When I was in London,' one of the gentleman told, 'I went to a party in a big house at Twickenham. It was the dead of winter and all night there was a nightingale twittering away in one of the trees in the garden. I'd never heard anything like it. It was amazing. All the guests went out in troops to listen, it was such a wonder. Only later I found out it was a lark – I mean, some bird-imitator from the music-halls had been hired to sit up there and do it, all rugged up against the cold, poor chap, and blowing on his fingers when he wasn't being a nightingale. It's a wonder he didn't freeze.'

Europe, Jim decided, must be a mad place. And now they said there was to be a war.

He sat apart with his back to a tree and ate the sandwiches he had brought while the others had their spread. Ashley carried a glass of champagne across to him and sat for a bit, with his own glass, but they didn't speak.

Later, when he handed the ladies down on to the wooden landing stage he had constructed, at the end of a twenty-foot cat-walk, each of them said 'Thank you Jim,' and the gentlemen tipped him. Ashley never said thank you, and he pretended not to see the coins that passed, though he wouldn't have deprived Jim of the extra shillings by forbidding it.

Ashley didn't have to thank him. And not at all because Jim was only doing what he was employed to do.

At either end of the boat they held a balance. That was so clear there was no need to state it. There was no need in fact to make any statement at all. But when Ashley wanted someone to talk to, he would come down to where Jim was making a raft of reeds to attract whistlers, or laying out seed, and talk six to the dozen, and in such an incomprehensible rush of syllables that Jim, often, could make neither head nor tail of it, though he didn't mind. Ashley too was an enthusiast, but not a quiet one. Jim understood that, even if he never did grasp what Wagner was – something musical, though not of his sort; and when Ashley gave up words altogether and came to whistling, he was glad to be relieved at last of even pretending to follow. Ashley's talk was one kind of music and the tuneless whistling another. What Ashley was doing, Jim saw, was expressing something essential to himself, like the 'sweet pretty creature' of the willy wagtails (which didn't mean that either). Having accepted the one he could easily accept the other.

Ashley did not present a mystery to Jim, though he did not comprehend him. They were alike and different, that's all, and never so close as when Ashley, watching, chattered away, whistled, chattered again, and then just sat, easily contained in their double silence.

5

The war did come, in mid-August, but quietly, the echo of a shot that had been fired months back and had taken all this time to come round the world and reach them.

Jim happened to be in Brisbane to buy developing paper and dry plates for Miss Harcourt and new boots for himself. By mid-afternoon the news had passed from mouth to mouth all over the city and newsboys were soon crying it at street corners. War! War! It was already several days old, over there, in countries to which they were not linked, and now it had come here.

Some people seemed elated, others stunned. The man at the photography shop, who was some sort of foreigner with a drooping moustache and a bald skull and side-tufts, shook his head as he prepared Jim's parcel. 'A bad business,' he said, 'a catastrophe. Madness!'

Maybe, Jim thought, he had relatives there who would be involved.

'I'm a Swede,' the man told him, Jim didn't know

why. He had never said anything like that before.

But others were filled with excitement.

'Imagine,' a girl with very bright eyes said to him at the saddlers where he got his boots. 'I reckon you'll be joining up.'

'Why?' he asked in a last moment of innocence. It hadn't even occurred to him.

The girl's eyes hardened. 'Well I would,' she said fiercely, 'if I was a man. I'd want to be in it. It's an opportunity.' She spoke passionately, bitterly even, but whether at his inadequacy or her own he couldn't tell.

When he stepped out of the shop with his new boots creaking and the old ones in a box under his arm he saw that the streets were, in fact, filled with an odd electricity, as if, while he was inside, a quick storm had come up and equally swiftly passed, changing the sky and setting the pavements, the window-panes, the flanks of passing vehicles in a new and more vivid light. They might have entered a different day, and he wondered if there really had been a change of weather or he only saw the change now because that girl had planted some seed of excitement in him whose sudden blooming here in the open air cast its own reflection on things. He felt panicky. It was as if the ground before him, that had only minutes ago stretched away to a clear future, had suddenly tilted in the direction of Europe, in the direction of *events*, and they were all now on a dangerous slope. That was the impression people gave him. That they were sliding. There was, in all this excitement, an alarming sense that they might be at the beginning of a stampede.

He went into the Lands Office Hotel for a quiet beer; it was where he usually went; it was the least rowdy of the Brisbane pubs.

He found it full of youths who would normally have been at work at this hour in government offices or insurance buildings or shops. They were shouting one another rounds, swaggering a little, swapping boasts, already a solid company or platoon, with a boldness that came from their suddenly being many; and all with their arms around one another's shoulders, hanging on against the slope.

When he went into the back for a piss, one of them, one of the loudest, was leaning with his head on his arm above the tiled wall of the urinal, his body at a forward angle. He seemed to have been like that for a long time.

'Are you alright?' Jim enquired.

'Yes, mate, I'm alright,' the youth said mildly. He tilted himself upright, buttoned up and staggered away. Outside Jim saw him arguing with another fellow, his face very fierce, his fist hammering the other fellow in the upper arm with short hard jabs, the other laughing and pushing him off.

Later, round at the Criterion, it was the same. These were fellows from the law-courts, clerks mostly, wearing three-piece suits, but also noisy. Jim took one look and slipped into the ladies' lounge with its velvet drapes and mirrors, its big glossy-leafed plants in jardinières. He had never dared before. All this excitement had made him bold, but given him at the same time a wish for something softer than the assertions and oaths of the public bar. He met a girl – a woman really – with buttoned boots and a red blouse.

'Are you joining up too?' she asked.

'I dunno,' he lied.

She summed him up quickly. 'From the country?'

'No,' he said, 'the coast.'

'Oh,' she said, but didn't see the difference.

They got talking, and on the assumption that he too was off to the other side of the world and would need something to remember before he went, she invited him to go home with her. He wasn't surprised, he had known all along that this was where their conversation would lead. She was a warm, sandy-headed girl with a sense of humour, inclined to jolly her young men along. She looked at him quizzically and didn't quite understand, but was used to that; young fellows were so different, and so much the same. She touched his hand.

'It's alright. I won't bite, you know.'

He finished his drink slowly, he wasn't in a hurry; feeling quite steady and sure of himself, even on this new ground. Perhaps it was an alternative.

'Right then,' he said, and she gave a wide smile.

Outside the lights were on and there were crowds. Walking up Queen Street they found that in the windows of some of the bigger shops, the department stores where your cash flew about overhead in metal capsules, there were pictures of the King and Queen with crossed flags on either side, one Australian, the other the Union Jack. And the streets did feel different. As if they had finally come into the real world at last, or caught up, after so long, with their own century.

Taking a short tram-ride over the bridge, they walked past palm-trees and Moreton Bay figs till they came to a park, and then, among a row of weatherboard houses, to a big rooming-house with a lattice-work verandah. He waited on the step while the girl plunged into her leather handbag after the key, and his eye was led, among the huge trunks of the Moreton Bay figs down in the park, to a scatter of glowing points that could have been fireflies, but were, of course, cigarettes. There was some sort of gathering. Suddenly, before the girl could turn her key in the lock, the stillness was broken by a vicious burst of sound, a woman shrieking, then the curses of more than one man.

'Oh,' she said, surprised that he should have stopped and turned, 'abos!' Then repeated it as if he hadn't understood. 'Abos!'

There was an explosion. Breaking glass. A bottle had been dashed against a tree-trunk, and a figure staggered out into the glow of the streetlamp, a black silhouette that became a white-shirted man with his hands over his face and blood between them. He weaved about, but very lightly. He might have been executing a graceful dance, all on his own there, till another figure, hurling itself from the shadows, brought him down. There were thumps. A woman's raucous laughter.

'Abos,' the girl said again with cool disgust, as if the

rituals being enacted, however violent, and in whatever degenerate form, were ordinary and not to be taken note of. 'Aren't you coming in then? Slowcoach!'

Her name was Connie. Jim was quite pleased with himself, and with her as well. Walking back afterwards, in the early evening, with the town very lively still and a lot of young fellows standing about drunk under lampposts, some of them with girls but always talking excitedly to one another, he was able to take all this *action* more easily. Maybe it concerned him, maybe it didn't. So much of what a man was existed within and was known only to himself, and to those, even strangers, to whom he might occasionally, slowly, reveal it.

He stood at the entrance to the bridge and watched the dark waters of the river swarming with lights and saw the butt of his cigarette, glowing all the way, make a wide arc towards it. Nothing had changed.

But back at the boarding house where he usually stayed, he was wakened not long after he fell asleep by a great noise in the street below, and going with one or two others to the balcony, saw a procession making its way towards them of what looked like thousands. He had never seen so many people in one place before.

They were young men mostly, and some were in uniform, a group of naval ensigns; but there were also women of all ages, and they were all shouting and cheering and offering up snatches of song. At the head of the crowd, on the shoulders of one of the white-suited navy boys, was a little fair-headed lad in a kilt, who was waving his arms about among the flags. He seemed significant in some way – the crowd had chosen him as a symbol – and Jim felt disturbed; he couldn't have said why. Maybe it was the hour. The loose excitement that had been about all day, and had found no focus, had gathered itself to a head at last and was careering through the streets, sweeping everything before it. Sleepy Brisbane! It might be Paris or somewhere, with all these people surging about in the middle of the night, marching with linked arms and chanting slogans. Crowds made him nervous. *Is this what it will be like from now on*? he asked himself. *Will I get used to it*?

One of the old-timers who shared the room with him explained. They were coming, this great press of people, from the Market square, where they had gathered to hear an address from the Lord Mayor. Those noisy outriders of the procession, blatant youths waving scraps of paper, were those who had been enrolled earlier in the evening at the Town Hall, over five hundred they said, and considered themselves to be soldiers already and therefore released from civilian restraint. They were at war.

Jim looked, and wondered if his certainty of a little earlier, that he need not be concerned, would hold. When he went back to bed he couldn't sleep. Far off, the crowd was still spasmodically sending up faint hurrahs, and scraps of tunes, half-familiar, came to his ear: *The Boys of the Old Brigade* – they liked that one, they sang it twice – and more solemnly, *God Save the King*. Lying back with his arms folded under his head, an ordinary if unpatriotic stance, he could imagine all those others falling still and coming to attention as they sang. It might, after all, be serious.

In the morning, as he buttoned his shirt at the window, he looked again at the street where the procession had passed – it was littered with tramtickets and sheets of trampled newspaper that sailed in the westerly – then across the flat, weatherboard city to the hills. By midday he was home.

'Anything much going on in Brisbane?' Miss Harcourt enquired.

'Well,' Jim said, 'you know. The war. Not much otherwise.'

Miss Harcourt looked concerned for a moment and he thought she too might ask if he would go. But she didn't.

Jim stroked his upper lip, where for two days now he had been nursing the beginning of a moustache.

6

They were the days of the big migrations, those last days of August and early September, and Jim spent long hours observing and noting down new arrivals: the first *refugees* Miss Harcourt called them – a strange word, he wondered where she had heard it. He never had.

Tree martins first, but they came only from the Islands and they came to breed; great flocks of them were suddenly there overnight, already engaged in re-making old nests; dotterel and grey-crowned knots, the various tattlers; once a lone greenshank; then sharp-tailed sandpipers, wood sandpipers from the Balkans, whimbrel, grey plover, the Eastern Curlew, Japanese snipe, fork-tailed swifts from Siberia; then much later, towards the turn of the year, Terek sandpipers and pratincoles, the foreign ones in the same flock with locals but clearly distinguishable. He filled book after book with his sightings, carefully noting the numbers and dates of arrival.

The first sight of a bird, there again, after so many months' absence, in the clear round of his glasses, with a bit of local landscape behind it, a grass tuft or reeds or a raft of sticks – that was the small excitement. Quickly he took from his pocket the folded notebook with its red oilcloth cover and the pencil stub from behind his ear, and with his eye still on the bird, made his illegible scribbles. The greater excitement was in inscribing what he had seen into The Book.

Using his best copybook hand, including all the swirls and hooks and tails on the capital letters that you left off when you were simply jotting things down, he entered them up, four or five to a page. This sort of writing was serious. It was giving the creature, through its name, a permanent place in the world, as Miss Harcourt did through pictures. The names were magical. They had behind them, each one, in a way that still seemed mysterious to him, as it had when he first learned to say them over in his head, both the real bird he had sighted, with its peculiar markings and its individual cry, and the species with all its characteristics of diet, habits, preference for this or that habitat, kind of nest, number of eggs etc. Out of air and water they passed through their name, and his hand as he carefully formed its letters, into The Book. Making a place for them there was giving them existence in another form, recognizing their place in the landscape, or his stretch of it: providing 'sanctuary'.

He did his entering up at a particular time and in a particular frame of mind. He liked to have the lamp set just so, and chose a good pen and the best ink; bringing to the occasion his fullest attention; concentrating, as he had on those long boring afternoons at the one teacher school when he had first, rather reluctantly and without at all knowing what it was to be for, learned to form the round, full-bodied letters; and adding with a flourish now the crosses of the big F's, the curled tails of the Q's. He was proud of his work, and pleased when, each week, he was able to show Ashley what he had added.

'Beautiful!' Ashley said for the names, the writing, as he never did for the actual birds, to which he brought only his silence. And that was right. It pleased Jim to have the verbal praise for The Book and silence in the face of the real creature as it lifted its perfect weight from water into air, since in that way Ashley's reaction mirrored his own.

When Ashley and Julia Bell were married at the end of the year Jim presented them with the first of the Books; not exactly as a wedding gift, since that would have been presumptuous, and anyway, the Book was Ashley's already, but as a mark of the occasion. With it went the first of Miss Harcourt's pictures.

7

It was just before that, in late November, that Jim caught one day, in a casual sweep of his glasses over a marshy bank, a creature that he recognized and then didn't: the beak was too long and down-curved, the body too large for any of the various sandpipers. He stared and didn't know what it was. He couldn't have been more puzzled, more astonished, if he'd found a unicorn.

Next day, just on the offchance, he took Miss Harcourt to the place and they waited, silent for the most part, and talking about nothing much when they did talk, while Jim covered the area with his glasses.

Miss Harcourt rather sprawled, with her boots at the end of outstretched legs and her great skirt rumpled, not at all minding the dust. Her bonnet was always lopsided and she didn't mind that either. She had her own rules and kept them but she didn't care for other people's. Jim's father thought her mad: 'That old girl you hang about with,' he sneered 'she's a bit of a hatter.' But she spoke like a lady, she didn't hit the bottle and had, except for her passion for photography and the equipment she lugged about, no visible eccentricities. People found her, as a subject for gossip, unmanageable, unrewarding, and she oughtn't to have been; they resented it. So his father and some others called her mad but could not furnish evidence. She refused to become a character. In the end they left her alone.

Jim chewed a match, working it round and round his jaw.

At last it was there. It had stepped right out of cover into a break between reeds. Raising a finger to warn her, he passed the field-glasses.

'By that clump of reeds,' he whispered, 'at ten o'clock.'

She took the glasses, drew herself up with some difficulty, and looked. She gave a little gasp that filled out and became a sigh, a soft 'Ooooh'.

'What is it?'

She sat back and lowered the glasses to her lap.

'Jim,' she said, 'it's a dunlin. You couldn't miss it. They used to come in thousands back home, all along the shore and in the marshes. Common as starlings.'

He took the glasses and stared at this rare creature he had never laid eyes on till yesterday that was as common as a starling.

'Dunlin,' he said.

And immediately on his lips it sounded different, and it wasn't just the vowel. She could have laughed outright at the newness of the old word now that it had arrived on this side of the globe, at its difference in his mouth and hers.

'But *here,*' he said.

He raised the glasses again.

'It doesn't occur.'

But it was there just the same, moving easily about and quite unconscious that it had broken some barrier that might have been laid down a million years ago, in the Pleiocene, when the ice came and the birds found ways out and since then had kept to the same ways. Only this bird hadn't.

'Where does it come from?'

'Sweden. The Baltic. Iceland. Looks like another refugee.'

He knew the word now. Just a few months after he first heard it, it was common, you saw it in the papers every day.

'Tomorrow,' he said, 'we should try and get a photograph. Imagine if it's the very first.' He longed to observe the squat body in flight, to see the wing-formation and the colour of the underwings and the method of it, which had brought the creature, alone of its kind, so far out of the way. But he didn't want it to move. Not till they'd got the photo. He kept the bird in his glasses, as if he could hold it there, on that patch of home ground, so long as he was still looking, the frame of the lens being also in some way magical, a boundary it would find it difficult to cross. He was sweating with the effort, drawing sharp breaths. At last, after a long time, he didn't know how long, he laid the glasses regretfully aside and found Miss Harcourt regarding him with a smile.

'What's the matter?' he said self-consciously, aware

that his intensity sometimes made him a fool.

'Nothing, Jim. Nothing's the matter.'

She had been watching him as closely as he had watched the bird.

Next day she came with her equipment, her 'instruments of martyrdom' she called them, and took the photograph. It wasn't difficult. Jim sat, when it was developed, and stared. It seemed odd to her that it should be so extraordinary, though it was of course, this common little visitor to the shores of her childhood, with its grating cry that in summers back there she would, before it was gone, grow weary of, which here was so exotic, and to him so precious. The way he was clutching the picture! She was amazed by this new vision of him, his determination, his intensity.

'I was the first to see it,' he told her, 'I must be, or someone would have left a record. Miss Harcourt, we've discovered something!'

Rediscovered, she might have said, speaking for her own experience; but was moved just the same to be included.

The most ordinary thing in the world.

She had come so far to where everything was reversed that even that didn't surprise her.

8

One day Bert, Ashley Crowther's aviator friend, offered to take Jim up for a 'spin'.

Jim hesitated, but recognizing that it was really Ashley's doing, and had been intended as a gift, he felt he couldn't refuse, though he had no real curiosity about how things would look from above. New views of things didn't interest him, and he realized, now that it was about to happen, that he had a blood fear, a bone fear, of leaving the earth, some sense, narrow and primitive, derived maybe from a nightmare he had forgotten but not outgrown, that the earth was man's sphere and the air was for the birds, and that though man might break out of whatever bounds had been set him, and in doing so win a kind of glory, it was none the less a stepping out of himself that would lead to no good. Jim was conservative. He preferred to move at ground level. When he raised his eyes skyward it was to wonder at creatures who were other than himself.

But he appeared at the appointed time in the big paddock beyond the house, with his hands in his pockets, his jaw set, and his hat pulled down hard on his brow.

The flying machine sat among cow-pats casting a squat shadow. It had two planes mounted one above the other and four booms leading out to the tail, which was a box affair with rudders. The place where you sat (there was room for two sitting in tandem) was on the main plane, and the whole thing, as if no one had considered at the beginning how to hold all the various bits of it together, was crossed and criss-crossed with piano-wire. It looked improvised, as if Bert had put it together especially for the occasion. Jim saw nothing in it that suggested flight, no attempt to reproduce in wood, canvas, metal, the beauty of the bird. It looked more like a monstrous cage, and he wasn't at all surprised to hear Bert refer to it as 'the crate'.

Jim regarded it in a spirit of superstitious dread; and in fact these machines too, in the last months, had entered a new dimension. After just a few seasons of gliding over the hills casting unusual shadows and occasionally clipping the tops of trees, new toys of a boyish but innocent adventuring, they had changed their nature and become weapons. Already they were being used to drop bombs and had been organized, in Europe, into a new fighting arm. Bert was shortly to join such a force. In a week or two he would be sailing to England and soon afterwards might be flying over France. In the meantime they were in Ashley Crowther's dry paddock on a hot day towards the end of June. The air glittered and was still.

'Right you are Jim,' Bert said briskly. He was wearing goggles set far back on his head, which was covered with a leather skull-cap. He looked, Jim thought, with the round eyes set above his forehead, like some sort of cross between a man and a grasshopper. 'Just put these on, old fellow,' he said, offering Jim, with all the jolly camaraderie of a new mystery with its own jargon, and its own paraphernalia, the chance of a similar transformation, 'it's a bit breezy up there, and you'll want to see what there is to see, won't you? That's the whole point. Let me show you how to get in.'

Jim accepted the uniform, but felt too heavy for flight, as if he belonged to an earlier version of the species that would never make the crossing. Conscious of the weight of his boots, his hands, the bones in his pelvis, he climbed in behind Bert, terribly cramped in the narrow seat and already sweating. The breeze was singing in the wires, and it seemed to him for a moment that they were about to make their ascent in some sort of harp that they were taking up, for Ashley's amusement, to be played by the wind. *I know what fascinates Ashley*, he thought. *It's all this piano wire*!

'Good luck!' Ashley shouted, flapping his arms as if he might be about to take off under his own steam.

'Just relax,' Bert shouted. 'The machine does the flying. All we have to do is sit still. You're safe as houses in a crate like this.'

One of the boys from the sheds, who had been coming out to do this all year, gave the propellor a hard spin, the engine turned over, and they began to wobble forward over the coarse grass, gathered speed, ran the length of the paddock, and lifted gently at the last moment over a slip-rail fence, just failing, further on, to touch the top of a windbreak of ragged pines. They were up.

They made a great circuit of the local country, at one point crossing the border. They flew close up to the slopes of the Great Divide, saw a scatter of bright lakes to the south and big rivers down there, high to the point of flooding, rolling brown between cane fields, then turned, and there was the coast: white sand with an edge of lacy surf, then whitecaps in lines behind it, then limitless blue. Bert pointed out a racetrack, and at Southport there was the ferry-crossing and the pier, beyond it the Broadwater dotted with sails and the rip below Stradbroke Island. On the way back, flying lower, Jim had a clear view of what he had already seen in imagination: the swamp and its fringe of tea-tree forest; the paddocks, first green with underlying water then dry and scrubby, that sloped towards the jagged hills, and on the other side the dunes; the two forested hummocks that were Big and Little Burleigh; and a creek entering the sea over a sandbar, through channels of every depth of blue. It was all familiar. He had covered every inch of this country at ground level and had in his mind's eye a kind of map that was not very different from what now presented itself to the physical one. It was, if anything, confirmation; that what he had in his head was a true picture and that he need never go up again.

Once he realized this, and had passed his own test, he could relax and enjoy the sensation of just being there. It was exciting. Especially the rush of air.

But what came to him most clearly was how the map in his own head, which he had tested and found accurate, might be related to the one the birds carried in theirs, which allowed them to find their way – by landmarks, was it? – halfway across the world. It was the wonder of that, rather than the achievement of men in learning how to precipitate themselves into the air at sixty miles an hour, that he brought away from the occasion. And the heads so small!

So it did give him a new view after all.

'I believe you been up in one a' them machines,' his father taunted. 'I don't s'pose you seen any white feathers flyin' about up there. If you did I'd ask you where you reckon they might'v come from. An' I wasn't thinkin' v' angels. Nor Mrs 'Arvey's chooks neither.'

It was a time immediately after news had come of the landings at Gallipoli and the slaughter of the following weeks. People's attitude to the war was changing. Even his father, who hadn't been concerned at first, was suddenly fiercely patriotic and keen for battle. A new seriousness had entered their lives, which was measured by the numbers of the dead they suddenly knew, the fact that history was being made and that the names it threw up this time were their own. Neighbours had lost sons. Some of them were fellows Jim had been at school with. And his father felt, Jim thought, that his son ought to be lost as well. His father was bitter. Jim was depriving him of his chance to reach out and touch a unique thing, to feel that he too had dug into the new century and would not be repulsed.

'I'd go meself,' he insisted, 'if I wasn't so long in the tooth. To be with them *lads*! I'd give me right arm t' go!' And he punched hard at his open fist.

Only he wouldn't, Jim thought. He wouldn't be able to lift his left arm quick enough to keep up with his thirst.

Jim felt the ground tilting, as he had felt it that first day in Brisbane, to the place where the war was, and felt the drag upon him of all those deaths. The time would come when he wouldn't be able any longer to resist. He would slide with the rest. Down into the pit.

Later he was to think of that view from Bert's plane as his last vision of the world he knew, and of their momentarily losing sight of it when they turned to come down as the moment when he knew, quite certainly, that he would go. He didn't discuss it with anyone. But two weeks later, after having a few drinks in the pub and playing a slow game of pool, he rode up to Brisbane on the back of a fellow's motorbike – he didn't know the man, they had met only an hour before – and they both joined up.

If he didn't go, he had decided, he would never understand, when it was over, why his life and everything he had known were so changed, and nobody would be able to tell him. He would spend his whole life wondering what had happened to him and looking into the eyes of others to find out.

He strolled up to the house next morning and told Ashley Crowther. He didn't bother to tell his father.

Ashley nodded. They were sitting on their heels at the edge of the verandah, Jim chewing a match and Ashley, his eyes narrowed, gazing out over the paddocks, which glittered in the early morning chill. Now that the lower paddock had been ploughed and replanted, the Monuments could be seen, standing like ruined columns among the new shoots.

They didn't speak about Jim's work. It was left unstated that the job would be there for him when he got back. The birds could wait. The timespan for them was more or less infinite.

Miss Harcourt was not so easy. She seemed angry, but cheered up a little after they'd had tea.

'I'll hold the fort,' she said, making it sound the more heroic option.

He went the next day, and it was Miss Harcourt who rode up to the siding with him and waited to see him aboard. He stood looking at her out of the grimy window, her square grey figure among the coarse grass, with the smuts flying back in a cloud towards her as she swiftly receded. She was holding her bonnet on against the wind and clutching at it whenever she tried to raise her hand to wave.

Jim closed the window, already almost a soldier, and watched the beaten land go flat.

His father had got sentimental at the last. He had given Jim five quid and tried, as if he were still a child, to put his hand on the back of his neck, which was newly raw from the barber. It had made Jim, for a moment, see things differently, as if a line had been drawn between the past and what was to come, the two parts of his life, and he could look at all that other side clearly now that he was about to leave it. He still felt the weight of the old man's hand, its dry warmth, there on his neck and saw that his father would be alone now, maybe for good, and knew it. 'Agh!' he had said fiercely, 'you're the lucky one. To be goin'!'

Three months later, when his son was safely born, Ashley Crowther went as well, but as an officer, and in another division.

9

The world Jim found himself in was unlike anything he had ever known or imagined. It was as if he had taken a wrong turning in his sleep, arrived at the dark side of his head, and got stuck there.

Others were involved. Many thousands. And they were ordinary enough fellows like himself. They came from places back home with comfortable names like Samford and Bundaberg and Lismore over the border, and had obviously known similar lives since they spoke the same way he did and liked the same jokes and tunes. They were called Nobby Clarke, Blue Cotton, Jock McLaren, Cec Cope, Clem Battersby, and one of them was a stocky, curly-headed fellow called Clancy Parkett, who was always in trouble. He had first got into trouble on the induction course at Enoggera, then on the boat coming over, and had been in trouble ever since – he had slipped out with another bloke, on one of their first nights in France, and come back with two strangled chooks still flapping under his tunic. He knew some of the best stories Jim had ever heard, ran a poker school, and could down ten pints at a single session. Clancy teased Jim because Jim wanted, in his cautious way, to put every step down firmly and in the right place. Clancy was just the opposite. In real life, in Australia, he was an electrician.

Coming over on the *Borda*, and at Larkhill on Salisbury Plain while they were being trained and held back, there had been time enough to get to know one another and for every sort of hostility and friendship to develop. Jim made no close friends in the platoon, nobody special that is; but he thought of Clancy as someone he wouldn't want to be without. He might have been there always.

A lot of the men had wives and children and Jim had, over the months, seen their photographs and learned their names. Clancy had a List: addresses as well as names, which he flashed but never let you read. He also had stories about each of the women on his List – for a while he had done project jobs all over the southern part of the state – and Jim heard a good deal about a fisherman's wife up at the Passage, called Muriel, and others, a Pearl, a Maureen, at places like Warwick and Esk. It was the names of the places, as much as Clancy's ribald accounts of peace time philandering, that Jim liked to hear. It did him good, it kept the old life real; and he had no stories of his own to relate.

It was the same later when he and Bobby Cleese, after a trench raid, had spent a whole day and night together in a shell-hole in front of the lines, so close to the enemy out there that they could hear the striking of matches in the trenches up ahead and one man endlessly snuffling with a headcold. It was early February and the weather was freezing.

Bobby had talked of the Bay, in a low voiceless whisper that itself created mystery and made the familiar seem strange, as if dangerous or forbidden. He talked about fishing off Peel Island where the lepers were.

'Whiting now. that's a nice fish. Sweet. You can eat pounds of it if it's softly boiled with a white sauce and a bit of onion an' parsley in it. Bony, but. I saw a bloke choke once. It was horrible. The best place for whiting is over towards Redcliffe or round the point in Deception Bay. You ever been to Redcliffe, Jim? It's got a pier'.

Bobby's voice, white-breathed in the cold, evoked the whole blaze of the bay, faintly steaming (it would be summer there) in the heat before dawn, and Jim could see it, almost feel the warmth in his own bones, smell the dirty bilgewater in the bottom of the dinghy and feel fishscales drying and sticking to his feet. It was there, the Bay. It was daylight there. Even as they talked now, far out in no-man's land under the dangerous moon, it was dazzling with sunlight, or maybe building up to a storm that would only break in the late afternoon. Men would be out exercising greyhounds, and a milkcart with three metal cans might be starting on its rounds. Whiting, thousands of them, were swarming under the blue surface of Bob Cleese's eyes.

Jim would have liked then to speak of the swamp

and the big seas that would be running at this time of year, king tides they were called, all along the beaches, threatening to wash them away.

'Golly but I'm cold!' is what he muttered instead. The mud round the edge of the hole they were in was frozen solid. It had a razor-edge of dirty grey where the moon touched it. Ice. They were in mud to their knees and crouching.

'Tell us again, Bobby. About that bloke 'n the fish-bone. Deception.'

But more reassuring than all this – the places, the stories of a life that was continuous elsewhere – a kind of private reassurance for himself alone, was the presence of the birds, that allowed Jim to make a map in his head of how the parts of his life were connected, there and here, and to find his way back at times to a natural cycle of things that the birds still followed undisturbed.

Out on Salisbury Plain in the late summer and autumn there had been thousands of birds. And earlier in the year, when they first crossed the Channel, at le Havre, after the long train-trip from Marseilles, he had seen from the side of the ship a whole flock of sandpipers with their odd down-turned wings flying low over the greasy water, and among them, clearly distinguishable because so much bigger, knots, that would have been down from the arctic, their bodies reddish in that season – the same grey-crowned knots he might have seen along the coastal sandflats at home, arriving in spring and departing at the commencement of autumn, just as they did here. It was comforting to see the familiar creatures, who might come and go all that way across the globe in the natural course of their lives, and to see that they were barely touched by the activity around them: the ferries pouring out smoke, the big ironclads unloading, the cries, the blowing of whistles, the men marching down the gangplanks and forming up on the quay, the revving of lorries, panicky horses being winched down, rearing and neighing, the skirl of Highland bagpipes. He noted the cry of these local sandpipers: *kitty wiper, kitty wiper*, which was new, and below them the cry of the knot, so familiar that he felt his heart turn over and might have been back in the warm dunes, barefoot, and in sight of a long fold of surf. *Thu thu* it went, a soft whistling. Then, more quietly, *wut*. Very low, though his ears caught it.

Still eager in those first days, he jotted all this down to be described later to Miss Harcourt. 'I have seen the dunlin' he was able to tell her. He had had no notion, from their single specimen, what they would look like in numbers. 'A great flock,' he wrote, 'twisting this way and that, all at once, very precise, with all the undersides flashing white on the turn.'

Back again at le Havre – it was winter now and they were camped on a greasy plain outside the port – Jim had been 'picked' by a big fellow from another company whose name was Wizzer Green.

He had never seen the man before. He didn't know what he had done, maybe he had done nothing at all, but something in him offended Wizzer, and while they were still wrought up after the crossing and tired after being marched up, there had been a bit of a fracas in which Wizzer tripped Jim and then accused him of deliberately getting in the way. In a moment they were eye to eye and preparing to fight.

There were no heated words. Wizzer's contemptuous challenge hadn't been heard by anyone else. But he and Jim had, at first sight almost, got to the bottom of one another. It could happen, it seemed. Jim had found himself defending whatever it was in him that Wizzer rejected, and discovered that he needed this sudden, unexpected confrontation to see who he was and what he had to defend. Enemies, like friends, told you who you were. They faced one another with murder in their eyes and Jim was surprised by the black anger he was possessed by and the dull savagery he sensed in the other man, whose square clenched brows and fiercely grinding jaw reminded Jim of his father – reminded him because he came closer to his father's nature at that moment than he had ever thought possible.

It was Clancy who stepped between them, and before Jim knew quite what had happened it was Wizzer and Clancy who were slogging it out, but in a different spirit. Their violence was ordinary. They exchanged blows and insults and did and said all that was appropriate to such encounters, while other men gathered in a ring and cheered, but the occasion was not murderous as the earlier one had been. The others – all but Clancy – had backed away from that, recognizing a situation for which there were no rules.

The odd thing was that Wizzer seemed as relieved

as Jim to have the moment defused.

Clancy, who ended up merely clowning, got a black eye out of it and for days after he teased Jim and refused to let the matter drop.

'I'm wearing Jim Saddler's black eye,' he told people. But in no way suggested that Jim had ducked the issue; and nobody thought that. He had been ready enough to fight, ready even to kill.

Jim wondered about himself. When, afterwards, he left a wide circle round Wizzer Green, it wasn't out of timidity but from a wish not to be confronted with some depth in himself, and in the other man, that frightened him and which he did not understand.

10

They went up to Ballieul in cattle trucks, forty to a car. *Eight horses or forty men* the notice proclaimed. It seemed, even for the army, a rough equation and you wondered who had made it.

The loading took hours as the various companies were assembled beside their packs and then urged up into the wagons, the last men pushing in. It was cold at first, then hot, and the cars stank. Even after they had hung their packs up from hooks in the roof there wasn't enough room for them all to sit or sprawl. Many had to stand, pressed in hard against the walls.

These wagons had once taken cattle up to slaughter-houses. The old smell of the animals was still there in the wooden slats of the walls and in the scarred and trampled floor. They had gone up to the shambles in dumb terror. It was different with the men. After all those months in England, and the days in a holding camp at Ooostersteene, where they had been given gas-masks and taught to use them, they were impatient. Just to be moving was in itself something – that, and the knowledge that you were going to arrive at last at the war. One fellow played a mouth-organ and they had a sing-song. But as the hours passed, twenty, twenty-four, and their limbs began to cramp, and they dried out with the sweating, and were slaked with thirst, it too became intolerable, this next stage, and they longed to get down, it didn't matter where.

Still, it wasn't all bad. You could slide the door open once you had found a place to settle, and if you didn't mind the cold, and see what sort of country you were moving into. There were roads off in the distance, some of them newly made, each with its own traffic, horses, guns with a carriage and limber, motor-lorries, occasionally a tractor, and columns of men marching in both directions, with officers on horseback ranging between.

The train slowed many times and jolted to a halt, its wheels grinding, and there was silence for a bit before the men began to curse. Some of them climbed down to piss beside the line; their piss steamed. One or two ran off into the snow and squatted, there seemed to be loads of time; and had to be hauled up again when the train, unpredictably, moved off. Clancy Parkett decided to get some hot water for tea, and while the wagons were still rolling slowly forward, he and Jim, leaving their rifles, jumped down and jogged along the whole length of the train till they came to the engine. They were racing it. Running easily in the soft French snow. Fellows leaned out of the wagons cheering. When they got there at last, Clancy, who was a bit on the heavy side, was too breathless to speak. It was

Jim, as they still jogged alongside, who told the driver what they wanted and showed the billy.

He was a big fellow with goggles and a moustache, in a blue boiler-suit. A Scot. He thought it very comic to see them jogging along and Clancy so breathless. He called the fireman out to look at them. The fireman, all stripped and sweatily begrimed, laughed out of his blackened face.

But they got the water, took it, all steaming as it was, on the run, then waited beside the track for their wagon and its familiar faces to re-appear. Jim held up the billy as if it were some sort of trophy, and as each wagon rolled by the men in it chiacked or cheered.

Jim would never have done any of it alone; but with Clancy it seemed like an adventure, a time out of all this that he would remember and maybe tell: the time I raced the train up to Ballieul with Clancy Parkett – his breathless conversation with the engine driver, the moment of simply standing all aglow in the cold, a spectator, while the faces of the whole battalion passed before them, and the land behind dipping away, foreign, mysterious, in snowy folds, crossed by black highways and tracks but empty of habitation. The tea when they gulped it down in sweet, steamy mouthfuls was especially good.

They were approaching the front. It was a new landscape now, newly developed for the promotion of the war. There were emergency roads everywhere, cutting across what must once have been vineyards or beet-fields, metalled for motor vehicles and guns, cobbled or packed with dirt for the men, and they were all in use, with men on foot or on horseback moving in dense columns, mules, horsed wagons, guns. Everywhere along the way there were blacksmith shops and dumps for ammunition, guarded enclosures containing spools of cable and great wheels of barbed wire, duckboards, sandbags, planking, solid beech-slabs for the new-style all-weather roads they were laying further up. Tramtracks ran between the roads, and telegraph-cables criss-crossed the earth or were being prepared for with deep slits. It was all in a state of intense activity. Things were being organized, you saw, on a large scale and with impressive expertise, as in the interests of an ambitious commercial project, the result of progress, efficiency and the increased potential of the age.

When they got down at last, on the outskirts of Ballieul, in the middle of the new landscape, Jim realized what it was he had been reminded of. It was a picture he had been shown, away back in Sunday school, of the building of the pyramids.

Large numbers of men, all roped together, were hauling blocks of stone up a slope, yoked together in thousands like cattle and hauling the blocks from every point of the compass towards a great cone that was rising slowly out of the sands. The fair-headed girl who was their teacher (she was called Agnes McNeill and later married a school-teacher) had drawn a moral from the picture: the Pharaohs were cruel (if you looked close you could see the overseers' whips) and ungodly, and their project was monstrous. But Jim, seeing the thing perhaps from the wrong perspective, and with the eyes of another century, had been impressed, as he was impressed now by the movement he saw all about him, vast numbers of men engaged in an endeavour that was clearly equal in scale to anything the Pharaohs had imagined and of which he, Jim Saddler, was about to become part.

11

It was a quiet section of the front. They were billeted in an abandoned cotton mill close to the centre of town. Though Armentiers by then had been fought over and taken and then retaken, and was frequently bombarded, it still retained a measure of normality; it hadn't as yet been gas-shelled and was not deserted. Girls appeared at the factory gate each morning with trays of buns and coffee; there were half a dozen good estaminets and several brothels; peasants on the outskirts of the town were still growing cabbages or trying to raise a wheatcrop right up to where the trenches began.

They were the local people whose farms had been where the war now was. They hadn't all left and they weren't all grateful that their land was being defended against invaders. Mostly they just wanted the war to move away. They were grim, wooden-faced people in clothes as muddy and ragged as the soldiers', their feet sometimes in clogs but more often in bundles of rags. They stood about on the doorsteps of shattered houses, defending their property – a few chickens, a cow, a cellar full of dusty bottles – against the defenders, who were always on the lookout for something to eat or steal, or for a woman who could be induced into one of the dirty barns, or for any sort of mischief that would kill boredom and take their minds off what lay ahead.

There were several wars going on here, and different areas of hostility, not all of them official.

As for the townspeople, they were like townspeople everywhere. The war was good business. The girls who sold cakes outside the cotton factory were pretty. Their mothers kept bars. Their younger brothers, in the afternoon, went up through the support lines to sell papers.

On the last night before they went into the line (they were to go up on December 23rd and spend Christmas there) Clancy prevailed on Jim to break bounds and go to a village just out of town. It was two miles off over the snow. It wasn't much of a place now, and probably never had been, but a woman kept a good estaminet there, in the shell of a bombed out farm-house, with eggs and sometimes cognac, and Clancy was on close terms with her. Though they had only been here a couple of weeks she was already on the List. Her name was Monique.

'Come on, mate, be a devil,' Clancy urged. 'We might all be dead by Christmas.'

Teasing Jim amused him. After all these months of raw camp life Jim still existed in a world of his own, not withdrawn exactly but impenetrably private. He did everything with meticulous care and according to the strict order of the book as if there were some peculiar safety in it, cleaning and swaddling his rifle, polishing his boots, laying out his kit. The odd thing was that Clancy respected this. It was what he saw in Jim that was most likeable and attractive. His drawing him out was a way of having Jim dig his heels in and be most earnestly himself.

'I tell yer, mate, in this world you've got t' work round the edge of things, the law, the rules. Creep up from behind. The straight way through never got a man nowhere.'

Jim dug in. 'No, Clancy. I reckon I'll stay.'

'Well Monique'll be disappointed. I promised 'er you'd be along. My mate Jim, I said. Next time up I'll bring my mate Jim.'

'The Captain –'

'Aw, bugger the Captain. D'y' think he cares? He makes the rules with 'is tongue in 'is cheek, the way he expects us t' keep 'em. Grow up mate! This is the real world. We're not the only ones, y' know. Half the battalion'll be there.'

Jim relented. It was, after all, their last night and the immediate future was unpredictable. They set out; but hadn't gone more than a hundred yards when there was a call behind them.

'Hey Jim, Clancy, where yous goin'?'

It was Eric Sawney, a pale, sad youth who from their very first day in Thompson's Paddock had latched on to Clancy and whose doglike devotion was a company joke. Clancy had found no way of discouraging the boy. Short of downright brutality Eric was not to be put off.

'Shit!' he said now, 'it's bloody Eric. I thought we'd lost 'im. They ought t' make that kid a police-dog.'

'Were yous goin'?' Eric repeated.

Clancy stood tugging his ear. 'Nowhere much, mate. We're just walkin' down our meal.'

'You're goin' into town,' the boy said, 'yous can't fool me. Can't I come?'

'Now Eric. Town is out of bounds at this hour. You know that. What'd y' mother say?'

'I havn' got a mother.'

'Well yer auntie then.'

Eric stuck. His drawn face, always pale, assumed a hard white look. He set his jaw somewhere between stubbornness and the sulks. Snow was falling.

'You're underage,' Clancy said desperately. 'I bet you're not sixteen.'

'I am so too. I'm eighteen.'

'Oh Jesus,' Clancy moaned. 'Come on then. But try not t' start a box on, eh mate? Keep that fierce temper a' yours under a bit of control.'

Clancy winked at Jim and Eric fell in beside them. Other groups, muffled against the cold, were up ahead, trudging on through the mud. There were more behind.

Monique was so unlike what Jim might have predicted that he wondered later about Muriel from the Passage and Phyllis, and Betty and Irene. She was a heavy blond woman of maybe fifty, sadly voluptuous, with bruised lips. She welcomed them all, let Clancy pinch her, and spent the rest of the evening resting her comfortable bosom on the counter or pouring slow drinks. Before long there were twenty or thirty of them, and later as many again from the 43rd. Two younger women, just girls really, came in to help fetch and carry and an old grannie with no teeth handled a big black pan, cooking omelettes and *pommes frites*. Clancy drank spirits, Jim and Eric *vin blanc* with syrup.

'Jesus,' Clancy protested, 'what is this? A kiddies' birthday do?'

But Jim craved the sweetness. For some reason, up here, he couldn't get enough of it. He blushed now to be in the same boat as Eric, who was always childishly whining for cakes and buns and whose pockets were full of squares of half-melted chocolate in silver paper for which he traded even his tobacco ration.

It was warm after a while, what with the crowd and the grog and the smoke from the pan. A Frenchman played a squeezebox. Jim got mildly drunk and Clancy got very drunk. Eric, wrapped up in his greatcoat and with his babyish mouth ajar, fell peacefully asleep.

'There mate, doesn't that feel good now? – a nice crowd, a woman leanin' on the bar.' Clancy had a talent for creating minor festivals out of almost nothing at all. Jim felt a great affection for him. 'I mean it's somethin' to remember isn' it, when we're up there freezin' our balls off all through Christmas. I remember last Christmas, I –' and Clancy was off on one of his stories. As usual Jim was soon lost in it. The wonders of Clancy Parkett's life. Only suddenly it turned in a direction he hadn't expected.

'Knocked me back,' Clancy was saying of some girl Jim had never been told about before and who didn't figure in the List. She had slipped into this particular story by stealth. Jim wondered if he hadn't, under the effects of the wine and the heat and Clancy's familiar voice, dozed off for a minute and missed her entry, till he saw that she had been in Clancy's sights all along, over there at the edge of what he was telling. He had, in his roundabout way, been leading up to her, but at the same time ignoring her presence, while he occupied himself with other things: the car he had driven last year, the places he went. He gave up at last and confronted her. 'Margaret,' he said, as if calling her in. 'Margaret she was called,' and immediately reddened all the way to the roots of his hair. Jim was astonished. The story had become a confession. 'So there you are. I joined up the next day.'

Jim didn't know what to say. He wasn't used to this sort of thing. He took another long swig of the sickly drink, then pushed it away from him; he'd had enough. Clancy gave Eric a shove and the boy started awake, grinning, then slept again.

'C'mon tiger,' Clancy said, hauling him upwards. Eric's eyes were closed and he was smiling blissfully. 'At least,' Clancy said, regarding the boy, 'if he's goin' t' get killed f' Christmas he'll 'v been pissed once in his life. Y' reckon you can walk, mate?'

'I can walk,' the boy said with sudden belligerence.

'All right, keep y' shirt on! I only asked.'

Next evening, after a day of anxious preparation, of cleaning and checking their kit and simply hanging about waiting, they made their way into the lines.

12

Often, as Jim later discovered, you entered the war through an ordinary looking gap in a hedge. One minute you were in a ploughed field, with snowy troughs between ridges that marked old furrows and peasants off at the edge of it digging turnips or winter greens, and the next you were through the hedge and on duckboards, and although you could look back and still see farmers at work, or sullenly watching as the soldiers passed over their land and went slowly below ground, there was all the difference in the world between your state and theirs. They were in a field and very nearly at home. You were in the trench system that led to the war.

But at Armentiers, on that first occasion, you came to the war from the centre of town. Crossing Half-past Eleven Square (it was called that because the Town Hall clock had stopped at that hour during an early bombardment; everything here had been renamed and then named again, as places and streets, a copse, a farmhouse, yielded up their old history and entered the new) you turned left and went on across Barbed-wire Square till you came to a big red building called the Gum-boot Store. There, after being fitted out with rubber boots that went all the way to mid-thigh, and tramping about for a few minutes to get used to the things, you were led away into the grounds of another, larger building, this time of brick, that was an Asylum; and from there, via Lunatic Lane, into the lines. Lunatic Lane began as a cobbled street, then became dirt, and before you quite knew it you were on planks. From this point the duckboards, for all their twisting and turning, led straight to the war.

They began to move up just at dusk, and by the time night fell and the first flares became visible, throwing their yellow glare on the underside of clouds and falling at times in a shower of brilliant stars, they were in the support line, stumbling in the dark through a maze of communication trenches, round firebays and traverses, jostling water-bottles, messtins, entrenching tools, grunting with the effort of trying to keep up, and quite blind except for the warning passed back from man to man of a hole up ahead in the greasy duckboards – *But where? How far? Am I almost on it?* – or a wire obstacle overhead.

The deeper they went the worse it got. In places where seepage was bad the duckboards were a foot under water. Once a whole earthwall had fallen and the passage was so narrow they could barely squeeze through: the place had been hit by a 'minnie'. They met two stretcher bearers moving in the opposite direction with a man who screamed, and some of the moisture, Jim thought, as they brushed in passing, must be blood. They hurried to keep up with the man in front and were soon breathless and sweating, partly because of the cracking pace that was being set – the men up front must actually have been running – but also because they were so keyed-up and eager to get there at last and see what it was. Everything here was so new, and they didn't know what might happen next, and when it did happen, how they would meet it. There was no stopping. If a man paused to adjust his pack or got his rifle caught in an overhead entanglement the whole troop might take a wrong turning and be lost in the dark.

The smell too got worse as they pushed further towards it. It was the smell of damp earthwalls and rotting planks, of mud impregnated with gas, of decaying corpses that had fallen in earlier battles and been incorporated now into the system itself, occasionally pushing out a hand or a booted foot, all ragged and black, not quite ingested; of rat-droppings, and piss, and the unwashed bodies of the men they were relieving, who also smelled like corpses, and were, in their heavy-eyed weariness as they came out, quite unrecognizable, though many of them were known to Jim by sight and some of them even by name; the war seemed immediately to have transformed them. They had occupied these trenches for eleven days. 'It's not so bad,' some of them mumbled, and others, with more bravado, claimed it was a cakewalk. But they looked beaten just the same.

They stayed eleven days themselves, and though the smell did not lessen, they ceased to notice it; it was their own. They were no longer the 'Eggs a-cook' of the easy taunt: 'Verra nice, verra sweet, verra clean. Two for one.' They were soldiers like the rest. They were men.

For eleven days they dug in and maintained the position. That is, they bailed out foul water, relaid duckboards, filled and carried sandbags to repair the parapet, stood to for a few minutes just before dawn with their rifles at the ready, crouched on the firestep, waiting – the day's one recognition of the reality of battle – then stood down again and had breakfast. Some days it rained and they simply sat in the rain and slept afterwards in mud. Other days it was fine. Men dozed on the firestep, read, played pontoon, or hunted for lice in their shirts. They were always cold and they never got enough sleep. They saw planes passing over in twos and threes, and occasionally caught the edge of a dogfight. Big black cannisters appeared in the sky overhead, rolling over and over, very slowly, then taking a downward path; the earth shook. You got used to that, and to the din.

Jim never saw a German, though they were there alright. Snipers. One fellow, too cocky, had looked over the parapet twice, being dared, and had his head shot off. His name was Stan Mackay, and it worried Jim that he couldn't fit a face to the name even when Clancy described the man. He felt he ought to be able to do that at least. A fellow he had talked to more than once oughtn't to just go out like that without a face.

Snipers. Also machine-gunners.

One of them, who must have had a sense of

humour, could produce all sorts of jazz rhythms and odd syncopations as he 'played' the parapet. They got to know his touch. Parapet Joe he was called. He had managed, that fellow, to break through and establish himself as something more than the enemy. He had become an individual, who had then of course to have a name. Did he know he was called Parapet Joe? Jim wondered about this, and wondered, because of the name, what the fellow looked like. But it would have been fatal to try and find out.

One night, for several hours, there was a bombardment that had them all huddled together with their arms around their heads, not just trying to stop the noise but pretending, as children might, to be invisible.

But the real enemy, the one that challenged them day and night and kept them permanently weary, was the stinking water that seeped endlessly out of the walls and rose up round their boots as if the whole trench system in this part of the country were slowly going under. Occasionally it created cave-ins, bringing old horrors back into the light. The dead seemed close then; they had to stop their noses. Once, in heavy rain, a hand reached out and touched Jim on the back of the neck. 'Cut it out, Clancy,' he had protested, hunching closer to the wall; and was touched again. It was the earth behind him, quietly moving. Suddenly it collapsed, and a whole corpse lurched out of the wall and hurled itself upon him. He had to disguise his tendency to shake then, though the other fellows made a joke of it; and two or three times afterwards, when he dozed off, even in sunlight, he felt the same hand brush his neck with its long curling nail, and his scalp bristled. Once again the dead man turned in his sleep.

Water was the real enemy, endlessly sweating from the walls and gleaming between the duckboard-slats, or falling steadily as rain. It rotted and dislodged A-frames, it made the trench a muddy trough. They fought the water that made their feet rot, and the earth that refused to keep its shape or stay still, each day destroying what they had just repaired; they fought sleeplessness and the dull despair that came from that, and from their being, for the first time, grimily unwashed, and having body lice that bred in the seams of their clothes, and bit and itched and infected when you scratched; and rats in the same field-grey as the invisible enemy, that were as big as cats and utterly fearless, skittering over your face in the dark, leaping out of knapsacks, darting in to take the very crusts from under your nose. The rats were fat because they fed on corpses, burrowing right into a man's guts or tumbling about in dozens in the bellies of horses. They fed. Then they skittered over your face in the dark. The guns, Jim felt, he would get used to; and the snipers' bullets that buried themselves regularly in the mud of the parapet walls. They meant you were opposed to other men, much like yourself, and suffering the same hardships. But the rats were another species. And for him they were familiars of death, creatures of the underworld, as birds were of life and the air. To come to terms with the rats, and his deep disgust for them, he would have had to turn his whole world upside down.

All that first time up the line was like some crazy camping trip under nightmare conditions, not like a war. There was no fight. They weren't called upon in any way to have a go.

But even an invisible enemy could kill.

It happened out of the lines, when they went back into support. Their section of D company had spent a long afternoon unloading ammunition-boxes and carrying them up. They had removed their tunics, despite the cold, and scattered about in groups in the thin sunlight, relaxed in their shirtsleeves, were preparing for tea. Jim sat astride a blasted trunk and was buttering slabs of bread, dreamily spreading them thick with golden-green melon and lemon jam. His favourite. He was waiting for Clancy to come up with water, and had just glanced up and seen Clancy, with the billy in one hand and a couple of mugs hooked from the other, dancing along in his bow-legged way about ten yards off. Jim dipped his knife in the tin and dreamily spread jam, enjoying the way it went over the butter, almost transparent, and the promise of thick, golden-green sweetness.

Suddenly the breath was knocked out of him. He was lifted bodily into the air, as if the stump he was astride had bucked like an angry steer, and flung hard upon the earth. Wet clods and buttered bread rained all about him. He had seen and heard nothing. When he managed at last to sit up, drawing new breath into his lungs, his skin burned and the effect in his ear-drums was intolerable. He might have been halfway down a giant pipe that some fellow, some maniac, was belting over and over with a sledge hammer. *Thung. Thung. Thung*.

The ringing died away in time and he heard, from far off, but from very far off, a sound of screaming, and was surprised to see Eric Sawney, who had been nowhere in sight the moment before, not three yards away. His mouth was open and both his legs were off, one just above the knee, the other not far above the boot, which was lying on its own a little to the left. A pale fellow at any time, Eric was now the colour of butcher's paper, and the screams Jim could hear were coming from the hole of his mouth.

He became aware then of blood. He was lying in a pool of it. It must, he thought, be Eric's. It was very red, and when he put his hands down to raise himself from his half-sitting position, very sticky and warm.

Screams continued to come out of Eric, and when Jim got to his feet at last, unsteady but whole (his first thought was to stop Eric making that noise; only a second later did it occur to him that he should go to the boy's aid) he found that he was entirely covered with blood – his uniform, his face, his hair – he was drenched in it, it couldn't all be Eric's; and if it was his own he must be dead, and this standing up whole an illusion or the beginning of another life. The body's wholeness, he saw, was an image a man carried in his head. It might persist after the fact. He couldn't, in his stunned condition, puzzle this out. If it was the next life why could he hear Eric screaming out of the last one? And where was Clancy?

The truth hit him then with a force that was greater even than the breath from the 'minnie'. He tried to cry out but no sound came. It was hammered right back into his lungs and he thought he might choke on it.

Clancy had been blasted out of existence. It was Clancy's blood that covered him, and the strange slime that was all over him had nothing to do with being born into another life but was what had been scattered when Clancy was turned inside out.

He fell to his knees in the dirt and his screams came up without sound as a rush of vomit, and through it all he kept trying to cry out, till at last, after a few bubbly failures, his voice returned. He was still screaming when the others ran up.

He was ashamed then to have it revealed that he was quite unharmed, while Eric, who was merely dead white now and whimpering, had lost both his legs.

That was how the war first touched him. It was a month after they came over, a Saturday in February. He could never speak of it. And the hosing off never, in his own mind, left him clean. He woke from nightmares drenched in a wetness that dried and stuck and was more than his own sweat.

A few days later he went to sit with Eric at the hospital. He had never thought of Eric as anything but a nuisance, and remembered, a little regretfully now, how he and Clancy had tried to shake him off and how persistent he had been. But Clancy, behind a show of tolerant exasperation, had been fond of the boy, and Jim decided he ought, for Clancy's sake, to pay him a visit. He took a bar of chocolate. Eric accepted it meekly but without enthusiasm and hid it away under his pillow.

They talked about Clancy – there was nothing else – and he tried not to look at the place under the blanket where Eric's feet should have been, or at his pinched face. Eric looked scared, as if he were afraid of what might be done to him. *Isn't it done already*? Jim asked himself. *What more*?

'One thing I'm sorry about,' Eric said plaintively. 'I never learned to ride a bike.' He lay still with the pale sweat gathering on his upper lip. Then said abruptly: 'Listen, Jim, who's gunna look after me?'

'What?'

'When I get outa here. At home 'n all. I got no one. Just the fellers in the company, and none of 'em 'ave come to see me except you. I got nobody, not even an auntie. I'm an orfing. Who's gunna look after me, *back there*?'

The question was monstrous. Its largeness in the cramped space behind the screen, the way it lowered and made Eric sweat, the smallness of the boy's voice, as if even daring to ask might call down the wrath of unseen powers, put Jim into a panic. He didn't know the answer any more than Eric did and the question scared him. Faced with his losses, Eric had hit upon something fundamental. It was a question about the structure of the world they lived in and where they belonged in it, about who had power over them and what responsibility those agencies could be expected to assume. For all his childish petulance Eric had never been as helpless as he looked. His whining had been a weapon, and he had known how to make use of it. It was true that nobody paid any attention to him unless he wheedled and insisted and made a nuisance of himself, but the orphan had learned how to get what he needed: if not affection then at least a measure of tolerant regard. What scared him now was that people might simply walk off and forget him altogether. His view of things had been limited to those who stood in immediate relation to him, the matron at the orphanage, the sergeant and sergeant major, the sisters who ran the ward according to their own or the army's rules. Now he wanted to know what lay beyond.

'Who?' he insisted. The tip of his tongue appeared and passed very quickly over the dry lips.

Jim made a gesture. It was vague. 'Oh, they'll look after you alright Eric. They're bound to.'

But Eric was not convinced and Jim knew that his own hot panic had invaded the room. He wished Clancy was here. It was the sort of question Clancy might have been able to tackle; he had knocked about in the world and would have been bold enough to ask, and Jim saw that it was this capacity in Clancy that had constituted for Eric, as it had for him, the man's chief attraction: he knew his rights, he knew the ropes.

'I can't even stand up to take a piss,' Eric was telling him. The problem in Eric's mind was the number of years that might lie before him – sixty even. All those mornings when he would have to be helped into a chair.

'No,' Jim asserted, speaking now for the charity of

their people, 'they'll look after you alright.' He stood, preparing to leave.

'Y' reckon?'

'Of course they will.'

Eric shook his head. 'I don't know.'

'Wilya come again, Jim?' A fine line of sweat drops on the boy's upper lip gave him a phantom moustache. 'Wilya, Jim?' His voice sounded thin and far away.

Jim promised he would and meant it, but knew guiltily that he would not. It was Eric's questions he would be unable to face.

As he walked away the voice continued to call after him, aggrieved, insistent, 'Wilya, Jim'?. It was at first the voice of a child, and then, with hardly a change of tone, it was the voice of a querulous old man, who had asked for little and been given less and spent his whole life demanding his due.

Outside, for the first time since he was a kid, Jim cried, pushing his fists hard into his eye-sockets and trying to control his breath, and being startled – it was as if he had been taken over by some impersonal force that was weeping through him – by the harshness of his own sobs.

13

The air, even at knee height, was deadly. To be safe you had to stay at ground level on your belly, but safest of all was to be below ground altogether.

Breathless, and still trembling, his head numb with the noise that was rolling all about, Jim scrambled to the lip of the crater, and seeing even in the dark that there was no glint of water, went over the edge and slid. He struck something, another body, and recoiled. But in the sudden flash above the crater's rim saw that it was, after all, only a dead man. He had stopped being scared of the dead.

Making their way out here, crawling, moving on their knees, squirming at corpse level, they had seen dozens of unburied men, swollen black, their bellies burst, some with their pockets turned out white in the moonlight where the scavengers had been through. Jim had been happy to stay down among them while the air thumped and shuddered and occasional flashes revealed the thickets of barbed wire they had fallen among. The air was tormented. Dull axes might have been swinging down. An invisible forest, tree after tree, came crashing all about, you could feel the rush of breath as another giant hung a moment, severed from its roots, then slowly, but with gathering speed, came hurtling to the earth. Jim crawled among the dead. Occasionally one of them stirred and slithered forward; it was the only indication he had of there being others out here, still alive and moving on. There had been seventy of them at the start. But one of the officers who had brought them out was killed almost immediately and the other had got them lost. They were scattered all round among the wire and were no longer a group.

It was this sense of being alone out here that had broken him. That and a renewed burst of machine-gun fire that whipped up all the earth around and made an old corpse suddenly bounce and twitch. He had decided then that he'd had enough. He lay breathless for a moment, then slid into the shell-hole from which, he decided, he would not come out. He put his arms round his head, while the sky bumped and flickered and the deeper sound of shellfire was threaded through at moments with the chatter of the Maxims. He was out of it.

He lay back, breathing deep.

But now that he was safe again the wave of panic that had caught him up retreated a little and he saw that he would go back. He told himself that what he had stood quite well till just a moment ago he could stand again. Besides, it was dangerous to stay here and be left. He rolled on to his belly in a moving forward posture, gripped his rifle, and was about to spread his knees and push up over the rim, on to the live and dinning field, when his heel was caught from behind in an iron grip. He gave a yell, kicked out and tried to turn, and another hand grabbed his tunic. He was hauled back. He and his attacker rolled together towards the oozy bottom of the hole. Hoarsely protesting, punching out wildly in the dark, he began to fight.

It was eerie, nightmarish, to be fighting for your life like this in a shellhole out of the battle, and with an unknown assailant. They were locked fiercely, brutishly together, grunting strange words, trying to stagger upright enough to get the advantage, to get some force into their blows. The fight went on in the dark till they were groggily exhausted. Suddenly, in a flash of light, Jim saw who it was.

'Wizzer!' he found himself shouting as the man's hand continued to clutch at his throat, 'it's me, you mad bugger. Jim. A friend!' Wizzer seemed astonished. Falling back he threw Jim against the wall of the shell hole and Jim lay there, panting, with his heels dug in, and watched Wizzer draw a sweaty hand over his face, removing the mud. It was Wizzer alright, no doubt of it. Overhead the sky was split. A livid crack appeared in the continuity of things, a line of jagged light through which a new landscape might have been visible. The crack repeated itself as sound. Jim's head was split this time and the further landscape in there was impenetrably dark.

'What're you doing here?' Jim asked between breaths when they had recovered from this external assault.

Wizzer looked sly.

'What're you?'

Jim didn't know how to answer that.

'I sort of slipped,' he said.

Wizzer's face broke into a mocking grin, and Jim remembered with shame that only a few moments ago he had been cringing at the bottom of the hole with his head in his arms like a frightened child.

'You pulled me back,' he accused, suddenly misunderstood and self-righteous.

'Yair?'

'Listen Wizzer,' Jim began again, 'we've got t' get outa here and find the rest of the platoon.'

'Not me,' Wizzer said, springing to the alert. Just that, but Jim saw that he meant it, was in no way abashed, and assumed in his own frank admission of cowardice that they were two of a kind. Jim began to be alarmed. He tried in the dark to locate his rifle. He had stopped hearing the noise overhead. There were so many ways of being afraid; you couldn't be all of them at the same time.

'Listen Wizzer,' he said softly, as if reasoning with a child, 'this is serious. We're right out in the open here. Whatever happens we'll be for it. We're right out on our own.'

His fingers reached the rifle and he looked to the place where the sky began, wondering, if he took off, whether he could make it before Wizzer was on him again. He wanted nothing so much now as to be back where he had been ten minutes ago, in the thick of it. Scared silly, but not yet sullied.

Suddenly, alarmingly, Wizzer began to quake. His shoulders first, then his jaw. An odd moaning sound came from between the man's clenched teeth and Jim could see the whites of his eyes in the mud-streaked face. He had drawn himself up into a ball and was rocking back and forth, clenching his fists to his chest. His whole body was being shaken as by other, invisible hands.

Jim could have scrambled away without difficulty then, but was held. He felt a terrible temptation to join Wizzer in making that noise, in adding it to the whine and crack and thump of shellfire beyond the rim of the pit; it would be so liberating. But some sense of shame – for Wizzer, but also for himself – held him back from that and made it impossible also for him to slip away.

'This is terrible,' he said to nobody, standing upright now, knee-keep in the mud they had churned up. He didn't know what to do. Wizzer had subsided into choking sobs. The other had let him go.

'Listen Wizzer,' he said, 'I'm leaving now. Alright, mate? If you want to come with me we could go together. But it's alright if you don't.' He backed away to the wall of the hole and dug in ready to climb. 'Alright Wizzer? Alright?'

He felt desperately unhappy. He really did want Wizzer to come; it was the only way to wipe all this clean. He kept his eye on the man, who was still again, with his head lifted like an animal and keenly observing, as if Jim were doing something incomprehensibly strange. Jim eased himself up towards the edge of the pit. 'I wish,' he said, 'I wish you'd come Wizzer.' But the other man shook his head. With one last look backwards Jim rolled over and out, and was immediately back on the field, in that weird landscape as you saw it at belly level of wire entanglements, smashed trees, the knees of corpses, and other, living figures, some quite close, who were emerging like himself from shallow holes. He was back.

He began, half-crouching, to move ahead. It was like advancing into a bee-swarm. The air was alive with hot rushing bodies that knifed down and swung hissing round his ears.

'Is that you Jim?'

It was Bobby Cleese. He was never so glad to see anyone in his life.

He scrambled to Bobby's side and they started forward together, then with fiery stars chopping at the earth again, they fell, together with others, who had also appeared as if from nowhere, into a wet ditch. From there Jim could see more of their lot over to the right.

So he wasn't lost after all. He had found the company, and might have considered his time out of all this a dream, a fear of what he might do rather than what he had done, if it weren't for Wizzer. Wizzer's face, and Wizzer's grip on him when they had wrestled together in the mud, were too real, and too humbling in his memory, to be dismissed.

'I was scared silly back there,' he whispered into Bob Cleese's shoulder. He needed to go forward now with a clear conscience.

'*You* were scared,' Bob said, and they both giggled.

Jim felt himself delivered into his own hands again, clean and whole – what did it matter if he got killed? – and discovered a great warmth in his heart for this fellow Bob Cleese, whom he had barely known till now. He was a bee-keeper back home. That was all Jim knew of him. A thin, quiet fellow from Buderim, and it occurred to him as they lay there that they might understand one another pretty well if there was a time after this when they could talk. Everything here happened so quickly. Men presented themselves abruptly in the light of friends or enemies and before you knew what had happened they were gone. Wizzer! It was odd to recall that not much more than a year ago he had been waiting, in what he thought of as a hypnotized state, for life to declare itself to him and make its demands.

Meanwhile, one of the others in the ditch had turned out to be an officer. Jim didn't believe he had ever seen the boy before, but he must have; it was the light. He was one of those fellows who were always clean. Even out here in the mud he looked perfectly brushed and scrubbed. His round face shone.

'Listen men,' he whispered, lifting his chin. He seemed filled with boyish nobility, playing his part of the junior officer as he had learned from the stories in *Chums*. He was very convincing. 'We're going forward, right?'

'It's a mistake,' Jim thought, whose own youth lay so far back now that he could barely recall it. 'This kid can't be more than twelve years old.' But when the voice said 'Right men, now!' he rose up out of the ditch and followed.

The boy was immediately hit, punched in the belly by an invisible fist and propelled abruptly backward. He looked surprised. 'Unfair!' his blue eyes protested. 'I wasn't ready. Unfair!' He turned regretfully away, but Jim had no opportunity to see him fall. He had already thrown himself into yet another shallow hole and was, this time, with two quite different men. Bob Cleese was ahead somewhere, or maybe behind.

'Will it be like this,' he wondered, 'all the way to Berlin?'

It was later, after another brief rush forward, that he and Bobby Cleese found themselves in the same shell-hole and were stranded there all night and all the next day as well, not twenty feet from the German lines. So they did have time, after all, and that night, and all the next day, they could hear Germans shifting their feet on the duckboards, striking matches to light their pipes, rambling in their sleep, and behind them, in no man's land, their own wounded groaning or crying out for help. To shut out the sounds, and to keep their spirits up, Bob Cleese had told about the fishing at Deception in a low, calm voice that quieted in Jim a swarm of confused terrors and set them smokily asleep.

It might have seemed, as the day wore on, that they would never get out. But they forgot that as their limbs unfroze at last in the yellow sunlight. The smoke of cookfires trickled up. They smelled bacon. And men could be heard going about their peaceable daylight tasks. Birds appeared, and Jim shyly identified them. In the afternoon they slept. Once you put to one side the notion of the danger you were in, and the possibility when night returned of sudden death, it was almost idyllic that long afternoon in the sun and the whispered talk.

They got back that time. It was later, much later, in June, that Bobby Cleese died. But by then more than a third of the battalion had disappeared and been replaced. Jim was a veteran. He had fought in every part of the line around Armentiers: at Houplines on the L'Epinette salient, at Ploegsteert, at le Bizet. He had been in a great battle.

It was while they were at Pont de Nieppe, waiting to come up to the battle, that Bobby Cleese was killed. The Germans shelled their billets with gas-shells, first tear gas, then phosgene. There was utter confusion and they had to abandon the town and sleep in the fields. Bob Cleese got a bad dose but didn't die till two days later.

Jim's company, by then, had been led in the dark through a maze of trenches to their old position at Bunkhill Row, and it was from there, just before dawn, that he saw the mines go up. The whole earth suddenly quaked under their feet as if an express train were rushing along below. There was a mighty roar. A cloud that bore no relation to the sound began slowly to rise westward. Like a pink and yellow rose made of luminous dust, it bloomed above the skyline, and climbed and climbed, till the sky in that quarter was entirely choked. It turned grey, and its smell as it withered was of charred flesh. When the smoke dispersed at last the landscape on every side was touched with flame. One whole hillside, over towards Hollebeke, beyond what remained of Ploegsteert wood, lay open and aglow, as if the door of a blast furnace had been thrown open and the horizon all round was lit with the reflection of it. It was like the mouth of hell. They rose up on a signal and poured into it.

Two days later, when they pulled out of the lines again, Jim got permission to go up to the hospital and find Bob.

It was a fine warm day, and in the aftermath of something very like a victory a holiday atmosphere prevailed. Weary men were making their way back out of the lines and many were wounded; others, more cruelly maimed, rode in closed wagons and you could hear their groans; but they were moving away from the battle zone into cleaner air and a glimpse of green and that made all the difference. The great pall of yellow smoke that hung over the battle-lines was well behind them and the sky ahead was blue. Jim especially felt light-footed and easy, and was happy to be striding out on his own with a twelve-hour pass in his pocket and the prospect of seeing his friend. He walked at first, in a great press of men, then accepted a lift on the back of a lorry, then further along rode for a bit on one of the guns. He met a blond fellow with no teeth who tried to sell him a safety razor. Another bearded soldier, very dirty and with no distinguishing tabs on his uniform, which seemed all odds and ends of other men's castoffs, had a stack of things on a groundsheet whose praises he sang in a high sing-song voice like a spruiker at the Show. There was a Mills bomb, a Prussian helmet with a bullet-hole in it, two watches, one with a metal band, a blue neckerchief, a revolver, a torch and a very real-looking glass eye. Jim didn't want any of these things, nor the gold fillings the man showed him in his dirty palm, but he inspected them along with others and wondered that the man had time for so much private industry. He accepted another lift in a field ambulance and played a short game of blackjack with two stretcher-bearers, who lost a shilling apiece. It was when he got down from the ambulance, just on the outskirts of the hospital, that he saw the crowd, and approaching the edges of it and pushing through was presented with something marvellous.

The men who had been mining under Hill 60, just a few days earlier, had discovered the fossil of a prehistoric animal, a mammoth, together with the flints that had been used either to kill or to cut it up. Very carefully, in the rush to get the galleries finished before the Germans finished theirs (for the two lots of miners had for several weeks been tunnelling in one anothers' path) the fossil had been uncovered and brought out, and now, with the battle barely over and the dead still being counted (fifty thousand, they said, on the German side alone) it was waiting to be conveyed behind the lines and examined by experts.

It was a great wonder, and Jim stared along with the rest. A mammoth, thousands of years old. Thousands of years dead. It went back to the beginning, and was here, this giant beast that had fallen to his knees so long ago, among the recent dead, with the sharp little flints laid out beside it which were also a beginning. Looking at them made time seem meaningless. Jim raised his eyes to the faces – intent, puzzled, idly indifferent – of the other men who had been drawn here, but they seemed no better able to understand the thing than himself. Some of them had come directly from the lines. Turning aside a moment, they regarded the creature out of crusted eyes as if it were one of themselves: more bones. Others, who could look at things from the distance that came with a fresh uniform and the brief absence of vermin, might be seeing it as it was intended to be seen, a proof that even here among the horrors of battle a spirit of scientific enquiry could be pursued, its interests standing over and above the particular circumstances of war, speaking for a civilization that contained them all, British and German alike, and to which they would return when the fighting was done.

In a field tent up at the hospital, where the dying were kept apart from the rest, Bob Cleese was in the final stages, fevered beyond hope. Jim regarded him with horror and was ashamed that he should feel disgust. Under Bob's mild eyes, where the whiting had swarmed, gathered the yellow pints of fluid he was spewing up out of his lungs, four pints every hour for the past twenty-four. Jim stared and couldn't believe what he saw. Yellow, thick, foul-smelling, the stuff came pouring out, and poured and poured, while Bob's eyes bulged and he choked and groaned. At last a nurse came, and gently at first, then roughly, she pushed Jim away. The whole tent was filled with such cases. The noise and the smell were terrible. Only the dead were quiet, lying stiff and yellow on their frames. Outside at last, Jim staggered in the sunlight and gulped for breath. He began to walk back towards the front, under the great yellow pall that in all that quarter hung low over the earth.

That night they went back into the lines, and for five days and nights they dug in and defended themselves against counter attacks and were bombed and machine-gunned from planes and lived in the stench of the German dead. Two weeks later they were back. For eighteen days. They were half-crazy that time, and once, digging furiously, while the sky cracked and blazed and men all round were being sliced with shrapnel or, with an entrenching tool floating high above them, were lifted clean off their feet and suspended a moment in mid-air, Jim felt his shovel scrape against bone and slice clean through a skull. He heard teeth scrape against metal, and his own teeth ground in his head. But he dug just the same, and the corpse, which had been curled up knee to chin and fist to cheekbone was quickly uncovered and thrown aside.

He had begun to feel immeasurably old. Almost everyone he had known well in the company was gone now and had been twice replaced. The replacements came up in new uniforms, very nice, very sweet, very clean, and looked like play soldiers, utterly unreal, till they too took on the colour of the earth or sank below it. It was like living through whole generations. Even the names they had given to positions they had held a month before had been changed by the time they came back, as they had changed some names and inherited others from the men who went before. In rapid succession, generation after generation, they passed over the landscape. Marwood Copse one place was called, where not a stick remained of what might, months or centuries back, have been a densely-populated wood. When they entered the lines up at Ploegsteert and found the various trenches called Piccadilly, Hyde Park Corner, the Strand, it was to Jim, who had never seen London, as if this maze of muddy ditches was all that remained of a great city. Time, even in the dimension of his own life, had lost all meaning for him.

14

Going up now was a nightmare. It was late summer and the roads, in the scorching heat, were rivers of dust filled with the sound of feet falling on planks, the rumble of gun-carriages and lorries, the jingling of chains, the neighing of horses, a terrible clamour; and when the rain fell, and continued to fall as it did for days on end, they were a sea of mud into which everything was in danger of sinking without trace and which stank of what it had already swallowed, corpses, the bloated carcasses of mules, horses, men.

Packed again into a cattletruck, pushed in hard against the wall, in the smell of what he now understood, Jim had a fearful vision. It would go on forever. The war, or something like it with a different name, would go on growing out from here till the whole earth was involved; the immense and murderous machine that was in operation up ahead would require more and more men to work it, more and more blood to keep it running; it was no longer in control. The cattletrucks would keep on right across the century, and when there were no more young men to fill them they would be filled with the old, and with women and children. They had fallen, he and his contemporaries, into a dark pocket of time from which there was no escape.

Jim saw that he had been living, till he came here, in a state of dangerous innocence. The world when you looked from both sides was quite other than a placid, slow-moving dream, without change of climate or colour and with time and place for all. He had been blind.

It wasn't that violence had no part in what he had known back there; but he had believed it to be extraordinary. When he was fifteen years old his younger brother, who was riding on the guard of a harvester he was driving, and singing over the tops of the wheat in his babyish voice *I'm the king of the castle, you're the dirty rascal*, had suddenly lost his footing and tipped backwards into the blades. Jim had run a half mile through the swath he had cut in the standing grain with the image in his head of the child caught there among the smashed stalks and bloodied ears of wheat, and been unable when he arrived at the McLaren's door to get the image, it so filled him, into words. There were no words for it, then or ever, and the ones that came said nothing of the sound the metal had made striking the child's skull, or the shocking whiteness he had seen of stripped bone, and would never be fitted in any language to the inhuman shriek – he had thought it was some new and unknown bird entering the field – of the boy's first cry. It had gone down, that sound, to become part of what was unspoken between them at every meal so long as his mother was still living and they retained some notion of being a family. He had never been able to talk to her of it and she had died looking past him to the face of the younger boy; and still they hadn't talked.

There was that. And there was a kestrel he had found once with a tin tied to its leg, a rolled-up sardine-tin still with its key. He had wept with rage and pain at the cruelty of the thing, the mean and senseless cruelty. His hands had been torn by the bird, which couldn't distinguish between kindness and more cruelty, and afterwards when it flapped away he had sat with his bloodied hands between his knees and thought of his brother. *There*, something in him had said. *There*! But he had freed only one small life, and the kestrel, with the weight of the sardine-tin gone but still there, and the obscene rusty object lying in the dirt where Jim had kicked it, was too sick from starvation to do more than flop about in the grass and would only feebly recover its balance in the air.

That was how it was, even in sunlight. Even there.

What can stand, he asked himself, what can ever stand against it? A ploughed hillside with all the clods gleaming where the share had cut? A keen eye for the difference, minute but actual, between two species of wren that spoke for a whole history of divergent lives? Worth recording in all this? He no longer thought so. Nothing counted. The disintegrating power of that cruelty in metallic form, when it hurled itself against you, raised you aloft, thumped you down like a sack of grain, scattered you as bloody rain, or opened you up to its own infinite blackness – nothing stood before that. It was annihilating. It was all.

Last time he had come up here there had been peasants in the field. Now the area behind the lines was utterly blasted. The earth was one vast rag and bone shop, the scattered remains of both sides lay all over it: shell fragments and whole shells of every size, dangerously unexploded, old sandbags trodden into the mud, a clasp and length of webbing, the head of an entrenching tool, buckled snapshots, playing cards, cigarette packets, pages of cheap novels and leaflets printed in English, German, French, scraps of wrapping-paper, bent tableforks and spoons, odd tatters of cloth that might be field-grey or horizon-blue or khaki, you could no longer tell which; smashed water-bottles, dented cups, odd bits of humanity still adhering to metal or cloth or wood, or floating in the green scum of shell-holes or spewed up out of the mouths of rats. They made their way across it. Once again they dug in.

One day when his company was back in support he was sent out with a dozen others to look for firewood in what remained of a shattered forest. All the leaves had been blasted from the trees and they stood bare, their trunks snapped like matchwood, their branches jagged, split, or broken off raw and hanging. They were astonished, coming into a clearing at the centre of it, to see an old man in baggy pants and braces digging.

A grave it must be, Jim thought. When the man plunged his spade in for the last time and left it there it had the aspect of some weird, unhallowed cross.

But it wasn't a grave. The bit of earth he had dug was larger than a body would require.

The old man, who did not acknowledge their presence, had taken up a hoe and was preparing the earth in rows. It was the time for winter sowing, as any farmer among them would know, but it was a measure of the strangeness of all things here, of the inversion of all that was normal, that they saw immediately from what he was doing that the man was crazy. One of the fellows called out to him but he did not look up.

They moved round the edge of the wood gathering splinters for kindling, and Jim, as he stood watching the man for a moment with a great armful, thought of Miss Harcourt, whom he hadn't remembered for days now. There was something in the old man's movements as he stooped and pushed his thumbs into the earth, something in his refusal to accept the limiting nature of conditions, that vividly recalled her and for a moment lifted his spirits. So that later, by another reversal, whenever he thought of Miss Harcourt he was reminded of the man, stooped, pressing into the earth what might by now be a crop of French beans or turnips or beets; though in fact they never went back to the place – Jim didn't even know where it was, since they never saw a map – and he had no opportunity of observing what the old man had been planting or whether it had survived.

Shortly after that, however, to keep hold of himself and of the old life that he had come close to losing, he went back to his notes. Even here, in the thick of the fighting, there were birds. The need to record their presence imposed itself on him as a kind of duty.

Saturday: a wryneck, with its funny flight, up and down in waves, the banded tail quite clear.

Wednesday: larks, singing high up and tumbling, not at all scared by the sound of gunfire. Skylarks. They are so tame that when they are on the ground you can get real close and see the upswept crest. I am training myself to hear the different sound of their flight paths; the skylarks that fly straight up and tumble and the woodlarks that make loops like Bert in his plane. The songs are similar but different because of the path.

Friday: a yellow wagtail. Can it be? Like the yellow wagtail we saw once at Burleigh that Miss Harcourt photographed. I wish I had the picture to compare. The sound I remember quite well. *Tseep, tseep*. The same yellow stripe over the eye. Or have I forgotten?

It was by then October. One night, lying awake in the old cemetery where they were bivouacked, just outside Ypres, he saw great flocks of birds making their way south against the moon. Greylag geese. He heard their cries, high, high up, as they moved fast in clear echelons on their old course. When he fell asleep they were still flying, and when he woke it was to the first autumn rains. All the damp ground, with its toppled stones, was sodden, and the men, lying among them or already up and preparing to move, were covered with the thick Flemish mud that stretched now as far as the eye could see and entirely filled the view.

15

The men, having stacked their rifles in neat piles and removed their packs, were taking their rest beside the road or had staggered off to where yellow flags marked the newly-dug latrines.

It was all so orderly and followed so carefully what was laid down in the book that it was difficult to believe, till you saw the racked and weary faces of the men, or observed the pain with which they lowered themselves to the earth, that they had already marched twelve miles this morning and were at the end of their endurance; or till you saw the terrible traffic that was moving in the opposite direction – sleep-walking battle survivors, walking wounded, men hideously mutilated and bloody, in lorries, wagons, handcarts – that there was a battle raging up ahead and that these men were making towards it with all possible speed; that is, at the precise rate, three miles an hour, with ten minutes rest for every fifty moving, that was laid down for the exercise in the army manual. Ashley Crowther knew these things because he was an officer and it was his business to know. He looked and marvelled. First at the men's power to endure, then at the army's deep and awful wisdom in these matters: the logistics of battle and the precise breaking point of men.

The traffic moved in a long cloud. Brakes crashed, horsechains clattered, men in the death wagons groaned or screamed as the rigid wheels bumped over ruts. Officers shouted orders. His own men simply lay scattered about in the dusty grass at the side of the road; prone, sprawled, dead beat. Very nearly dead.

A little way back they had passed the ruins of a village and he had been surprised to see that there were still peasants about. He saw a boy of nine or ten, very pale with red hands, who milked a cow, resting his cropped head against the animal's sunken ribs as he pulled and pulled. Ashley had looked back over his shoulder at the scene, but the boy, who was used to this traffic, as was the cow, had not looked up.

Later, on the outskirts of another group of blasted farms, he saw a man mending a hoe. He had cut a new handle and was carefully shaping it with a knife, bent over his simple task and utterly absorbed, as if the road before him were empty and the sky overhead were also empty, not dense with smoky thunder or enlivened at odd, dangerous moments with wings. Did the man believe the coming battle was the end and that he might soon have need of the hoe?

That had been at their last resting-place; and Ashley, while he lay and smoked, had watched the man shape and test the handle, peeling off thin slivers and rubbing his broad thumb along the grain. He was still at it, minutes later, when they moved on.

There were so many worlds. They were all continuous with one another and went on simultaneously: that man's world, intent on his ancient business with the hoe; his own world, committed to bringing these men up to a battle; their worlds, each one, about which he could only guess.

They were resting now, given over as deeply and as quickly as possible to sleep. In three more minutes they would be lumbering out to take their places on the road. By morning –.

A few miles away, behind concrete emplacements, the machine guns were already set up waiting. The deadly sewing-machines were stitching their shrouds.

He was profoundly weary of all this. Once or twice during his years at Cambridge he had spent a hunting weekend at Gem Oliver's place in Shropshire. They had sat in bunkers in the woods while beaters drove the small game towards them, and fired and fired, watching the creatures spring up and turn somersaults in the air or roll away twitching. It was like that out here. The men, scarcely believing they could be walking upright at last, and in daylight, in a place where they had always gone on their bellies by night, would move in ragged lines towards the guns, and in a flickered chattering dream, as the bullets whipped the air all about them or following their own trajectory, passed magically through, would, after seconds some, and minutes others, go down in waves under the whistling blades and lie randomly about, as they did now in the relative quiet of the grass.

Ashley blew his whistle. Slowly, as in a dream, the men rose and stumbled into the road.

He was surprised as always, as they came to attention, to find that they harboured within them, these peaceable farmers, cattlemen, clerks, plumbers, pastry-cooks, ice-men, shop-assistants, and those who had never done more than hang about billiard parlours or carry tips to race-courses, or sport flash clothes in city pushes, the soldier – hard, reliable, efficient – they could so smartly become. The transformation was remarkable.

It wasn't simply the uniform, though that was the mark of it; or the creation through drilling of a general man from whom all private and personal qualities had been removed. The civilian in these men survived. You saw it in the way a man wore his hat, or in the bit of cloth he chose – an old shirt-tail or singlet, a roll of flannel, a sock – to protect the bolt of his rifle. You heard it in the individual tilt of his voice through even the most conventional order or response. It was the guarantee that they would, one day, cease to be soldiers and go back to being school-teachers, mechanics, factory-hands, race-course touts.

It had happened to him as well. He had quite unexpectedly discovered in himself, lurking there under the floral waistcoat and his grandfather's watch-chain, the lineaments of an officer. He was calm, he kept his head; he kept an eye out for his men; they trusted him. He was also extraordinarily lucky, and being lucky had seen many men over these months, whose luck wasn't as good as his own, go down. This new lot –

who started out now as he gave the signal and the line began to move – they too would go down. They were 'troops' who were about to be 'thrown in', 'men' in some general's larger plan, 're-enforcements', and would soon be 'casualties'. They were also Spud, Snow, Skeeter, Blue, Tommo. Even he had a nickname. It had emerged to surprise him with its correspondence to something deep within that he hadn't known was there till some wit, endowed with native cheek and a rare folk wisdom, had offered it to him as a gift. He was grateful. It was like a new identity. The war had remade him as it had remade these others. Not forever, but in a way he would never entirely outgrow.

Ashley, whose mind was of the generalizing sort, had seen quite clearly from the beginning that what was in process here was the emergence of a new set of conditions. Nothing after this would ever be the same. War was being developed as a branch of industry. Later, what had been learned on the battlefield would travel back, and industry from now on, maybe all life, would be organised like war. The coming battle would not be the end, even if it was decisive; it was another stage in the process.

It seemed more important than ever now to hang on to the names, the nicknames, including his own, and if his luck held, to go back. And having learned at last what the terms were – and in expiation of the blood that was on his hands – to resist.

16

Jim leaned, half-sitting, half-lying, against the wall of the ditch, glad to feel the earth against his cheek, and also his shoulder, as he waited rifle in hand for the whistle that would take them in.

They had come up in the dark following a white tape, and stakes, also white, that had been driven into the ground but washed out overnight by a storm. After weeks of hot dusty weather the rains had come and the earth was sodden and astream. Just an hour ago there had been a bombardment. So many men were killed in the rear line that the companies being held there had been brought up with the rest, and they were all packed now into the same narrow space, a terrible press of men, stunned, anxious, elated, solemnly waiting.

Jim looked down the line of men who half-stood, half-sprawled against the opposite wall. It was like seeing his own group repeated in a glass, or like looking at the wall itself, since the men, their uniforms all caked in mud, seemed little more in the dim light than another wall built up out of faces with deep ruts in them and rocklike, stubbled jaws, skin greasily shining where it was drawn over the skullbones, knuckles grained with dirt, coarse-grained necks above collars grimed at the edge, the cloth of the uniforms also coarse, and like the faces all of one colour, the earth-colour that allows a man to disappear un-noticed into the landscape, or to pass through, hunched shoulders, flexed knee and elbow, into a wall.

But the wall was in motion, even in its stillness. The bodies were not all here. His own wasn't. Some of them were in the past and in another country; others might already have leapt the next few minutes into the future, and were out in the firestorm, or had got beyond even that to some calm green day on the other side of it. Those who were stolidly here in the present had gone deep inside themselves and were coming to terms with the blood as it rolled round and round from skull to foot, still miraculously flowing in its old course; or with that coldness in the pit of the stomach that no rum could touch; or that shrinking in the groin as belts were tightened, that withdrawal of their own most private parts, that said: *No further, the line ends here*. They were communing with themselves in words out of old nursery prayers, naming the names of those they had been instructed to pray for, the loved-ones; they were coaxing themselves, cheering themselves up, using always their own names, but as they had heard it when they were so young that it still seemed new and un-repeatable; holding at bay on their breath that other form of words, the anti-breath of a backward-spelled charm, the no-name of extinction, that if allowed to take real shape there might make its way deep into the muscles or find a lurking place in the darkest cells. *No, I am not going to die.*

One fellow, with calm grey eyes and a thin mouth, was smoking. Pale clouds drifted before him, greyer than his face, and his eyes were like flints in a wall. He cupped his hand and drew again on the cloud-machine. Another long drift, smoky-grey. And behind it the hand that was square and solid earth.

I am getting too far ahead, Jim thought. *That is for later. I should get back to where I am.*

None of this came to him as so many words. He perceived it or it unfolded in him. What he saw in clear fact was a line of children, sleepily and soberly intent, who waited with their knees drawn up for a journey to resume after a minor halt. He thought that because the place where they were waiting had been a station on the line from Menin to Ypres. Children might once have waited here on slow trips to the city. He closed his eyes and could have slept.

He felt out of himself.

It wasn't the rum; there wasn't enough of it for that – one mouthful, warm as blood. He had felt this way before with odd parts of his body. His feet, for example. In the intense cold of the winter they had sometimes seemed a thousand miles off, ten thousand even, and quite beyond reach. He had thought of them as having got sick of all this, as having made their way home without him, and had imagined them leaving their bare prints on sand, among gull-feathers, cuttle-shells and the three-toed scratch marks of oystercatchers beside the surf.

This was different. It was the whole of him.

He was perfectly awake and clear-headed, aware of the rough cloth of his uniform, the weight of his pack, the sweat and stink of himself that was partly fear; but at the same time, even as he heard the whistle and rose to scramble over the lip of the ditch, taking the full weight of pack, rifle, uniform, boots, and moved on into the medley of sound, he was out of himself and floating, seeing the scene from high up as it might look from Bert's bi-plane, remote and silent. Perhaps he had, in some part of himself, taken on the nature of a bird; though it was with a human eye that he saw, and his body, still entirely his own, was lumbering along below, clearly perceptible as it leapt over potholes and stumbled past clods, in a breathless dream of black hail striking all about him and bodies springing backward or falling slowly from his side. There were no changes. But he moved in one place and saw things from another, and saw too, from up there, in a grand sweep, the whole landscape through which he was moving: the irregular lines of trenches that made no sense at ground level, the one he had left and the one, all staggered pill-boxes, that they were making for, where the machine guns were set that spilled out lines of fire and chop-chopped at the air. The land between, over which they were running, was all flooded ruts and holes, smashed branches, piles of shattered cement. But from high up, with all its irregularities ironed out, it might appear as a stretch of quite ordinary country, green in spots and sodden with rain, over which small creatures were incomprehensibly running and falling, a bunched and solid mass that began to break up and develop spaces like a thinning cloud.

He saw it all, and himself a distant, slow-moving figure within it: the long view of all their lives, including his own – all those who were running, half-crouched, towards the guns, and the men who were firing them; those who had fallen and were noisily dying; the new and the old dead; his own life neither more nor less important than the rest, even in his own vision of the thing, but unique because it was his head that contained it and in his view that all these balanced lives for a moment existed: the men going about their strange business of killing and being killed, but also the rats, the woodlice under logs, a snail that might be climbing up a stalk, quite deaf to the sounds of battle, an odd bird or two, like the couple of wheatears he had seen once in a field much like this, the male with his grey back and crown, the female brownish, who had spent a whole morning darting about on the open ground while he lay with a pair of borrowed field-glasses screwed into his head and lost himself in their little lives, in their ordinary domestic arrangements, as now, stumbling forward, he was, in a different way, lost in his own.

He continued to run. Astonished that he could hold all this in his head at the same time and how the map he carried there had so immensely expanded.

17

Suddenly, as it seemed, though several minutes must have passed, he found himself on the ground looking up at blue sky in which clouds moved so slowly that he blinked and then blinked again before he could be certain that they were not altogether stopped.

He drifted with them. He watched them tease out, sending long fingers into the blue, till the fingers, growing longer and thinner, dissolved and became part of whatever it was they were pointing to.

He blinked again. The sky had moved on.

Great continents now gave birth to islands in some longer process of time than he had been conscious of till now, and the islands too dissolved, like a pill developing fuzzy edges in a glass of water, then diminishing, diminishing. Soon they too had gone. Centuries it must have taken. When he blinked again it was quite a different day or year, or centuries had passed, he couldn't tell which. But he was aware now of the earth he was lying on. It was rolling.

He tried to push himself up on to one elbow so that

he could look about and see where he was. He was conscious of pain, far off over one of the horizons, but couldn't raise himself far enough to locate it. One of the horizons was his own chest. Beyond it a wan light flapped, as if a wounded bird threw faint colours from its wings as its blood beat feebly into the earth. There was nothing he could do about it.

Jim turned his head. Other figures were laid about on all sides of him, some of them groaning, others terribly stilled. He knew he should try to mark his position for the stretcher-bearers, and reached for his rifle which was away to the left; he tried, stretching his fingers, and in a slow access of pain he remembered fingers that had pointed and dissolved, and gazing out over the horizon of his shoulder at his own outstretched fingers, that were still inches from where the rifle lay, saw them too dissolve slowly into the earth, and closed his eyes and let them go. He felt the whole process, a coarsening of the grains out of which his flesh was composed, and their gradual loosening and falling away, as first his hand dissolved, then his arm, then his shoulder. If things went on like this there would be nothing left of him for the bearers to find.

He thought of the emergency field-dressing in the right flap of his tunic. If he worked quickly with his left hand, pulled the tabs and located the little white bag (he had been over all this a hundred times in imagination) he might be able to stop the process of his dissolving, but he would have first to find the place where it had started, the wound; and there was, strangely, not enough pain to give him a clue to where he was hit.

His head? His stomach? He thought of the yards of white bandage – two and a half to be precise – and as before, imagined himself wrapping it round his head. He wrapped and wrapped, the bandage seemed endless. There were thirteen thousand miles of it. It would stretch halfway round the world. To the Coast. To home. He began rolling it, slowly, carefully, in his mind, but before he had gone more than a few inches a feeling of drowsiness crept over him, a slow shadow as of the night, blurring the shape of things. It came over the edge of his body, moved into its hollows, muffled him in silence. He yielded himself up to it.

When he blinked again he was no longer under the sky. There was canvas overhead, and big shadows were moving across it, cast up by an acetylene flare. He was at ground level, far below, and through the open tent-flap came a cooling breeze.

It was crowded in here. But oddly silent. Other fellows, maimed and crudely bandaged, each with a white label tied to a button of his tunic, lay about on all sides, or sat up smoking, very pale and still, leaning together in groups. They had an air of eternal patience, these men; of having given themselves up utterly to a process of slow dissolution like the one he had observed in the sky and felt in his own body. Their eyes had the dumb, apologetic look he had seen in the eyes of horses who had fallen by the roadside and were waiting, without protest, to be shot. Their stillness, their docility, their denseness of flesh and rag and metal, made a sharp contrast with the shadows that moved about the walls of the tent and arched across the roof above them. They swooped and were gigantic. It was on them that the others, patiently, waited: to be touched and attended, to be raised.

Occasionally these shadows took on shape. A white-capped sister, a man in a butcher's apron all sopped with blood. Jim looked and there was a block where the man was working. He could smell it, and the eyes of the others, cowed as they were, took life as they fell upon it.

To his left, on the other side from the men who waited, who were mostly whole, lay the parts of men, the limbs. A jumbled pile.

I am in the wrong place, Jim thought. *I don't belong here. I never asked to be here. I should get going*.

He thought this, but knew that the look on his face must be the same look these other faces wore, anxious, submissive. They were a brotherhood. They had spent their whole life thus, a foot from the block and waiting, even in safe city streets and country yards, even at home in Australia. *Is that it*? Jim wondered. *Is that how it must always be*?

He turned to regard the man on his right, who was also laid out on a palliasse, and saw who it was.

How did he get here?

He closed his eyes. This was the place before the butcher's block. He did not want to be lifted up.

'Jim?'

He knew the voice.

'Jim Saddler?'

He was being called for the second time.

It was Ashley Crowther. He was there, just to the

right, also in the shambles. Jim blinked. It was Ashley alright. He was wearing a luggage-label like all the rest, tied with string to one of the buttons of his tunic.

He had seen Ashley twice since they came to France. Far back in the early days, when things were still quiet, their battalions had been in the same line, and they had stood together one day on a patch of waste-ground, on the same level, just as they might have stood at home, and had a smoke. It was a Sunday afternoon. Cold and still.

'Listen,' Ashley had said, 'band music.' And Jim, whose ears were keen enough to catch any birdcall but hadn't been aware of the music, heard it blowing faintly towards them from the enemy lines. Had it been there a moment before, or had Ashley somehow conjured it up?

'Von Suppe,' Ashley said, raising a finger to conduct the odd wavering sounds of Sunday afternoon brass.

'Listen' he said now, and his voice came closer. 'Can you hear me, Jim?'

The second occasion had been less than a month ago. They were way to the north, resting, and on the last night, after a whole day's drilling – for rest was just the name of another sort of activity, less dangerous but no less fatiguing than life in the lines – they were marched up the road to an abandoned château where several fellows were sitting about in the late light under trees and others were lining up at a makeshift estaminet.

A piano had been brought down from the château, a

big iron-framed upright with bronze candle-holders. It sat under the trees with a tarpaulin over it in case of rain. Several fellows, one after the other, sang popular songs and they all joined in and a redheaded sergeant from one of the English regiments played a solo on the mouth-organ. Later, a boy whose voice had still to break sang 'O for the wings of a Dove'; it was a sound of such purity, so high, so clear, that the whole orchard was stilled, a voice, neither male nor female, that was, when you lay back and closed your eyes, like the voice of an angel, though when you opened them again and looked, was climbing from the mouth of a child in a patched and ragged uniform no different from the rest, who stood bare-headed in the flickering light from the piano-sconces and when he had finished and unclasped his big hands seemed embarrassed by the emotion he had created, humbled by his own gift.

The concert went on in the dark. Jim heard a nightingale, then another, and tuned his ears, beyond the music, to that – though the music pleased him too; it was good to have both. He thought of Mrs McNamara's contention, so long ago, that it was the most beautiful of all birdsongs, and the other girl's regret that she had never heard it. Well, he had heard it. He was hearing it now. The trees, though they had been badly blasted, were in full leaf, and would in time, even with no one to tend them, bear fruit. It was their nature. Overhead, all upside down as was proper in these parts, were the stars. The guns sounded very far off. It was like summer thunder that you didn't have to concern yourself with: someone else's weather. Jim dozed off.

When he woke it was quite late and the crowd of men had thinned. Someone was playing the piano. Notes, he thought, that might have been taken over from the nightingale's song and elaborated, all tender trills. The strangeness of the place, the open air, or the keying up of his nerves in these last hours before going back, worked strangely upon him and he found himself powerfully affected. He sat up on one elbow and listened.

The music was neither gay nor sad, it didn't need to be either one or the other; it was like the language, beyond known speech, that birds use, which he felt painfully that he might reach out for now and comprehend; and if he did, however briefly, much would become clear to him that would otherwise stay hidden. He looked towards the square wooden frame like an altar with its flickering candles, and immediately recognised the man who was playing. It was Ashley Crowther.

He looked different, changed; Jim was astonished by him. It was as if the music drew him physically together. In the intensity of its occurrence at his finger-ends, his whole body – shoulders, neck, head – came to a kind of attention Jim had not seen there on previous occasions.

Now, still dressed in that new firmness of line, Ashley Crowther was here. His voice once again came close.

'Can you hear me, Jim?'

'Yes.'

He had in the middle of his forehead a small cross. A wound? The mark of Cain? Jim was puzzled. He had seen a man wounded like that, the body quite unmarked and just a small star-shaped hole in the middle of the forehead. Only this was a cross.

'Jim we've got to get out of here. I know the way. Are you strong enough to get up? I'll help you.'

'Yes,' Jim said, deciding to take the risk, and was aware in the darkness of a sudden hiss of breath that was his father's impatience.

He raised himself on his elbows. Ashley leaned down and put a hand under his arm. He was raised, but not towards the block. He stood and Ashley supported him. The relief he felt had something to do with the strength of Ashley's arm – who would ever have expected it? – but also with his own capacity, once more, to accept and trust.

'This way. No one will stop us.'

The nurses were too busy or too tired to observe what they were about, and the man in the bloody apron, all brilliant and deeply shadowed in the light of the flare, was fully engaged at the block. They walked right past them and out under the tent-flap into the night. Jim heaved a great sigh of relief. He too wore a label, its string twisted round one of his tunic buttons. He tore it roughly away now, button and all, and cast it into the mud. He wouldn't need an address label. Though Ashley, he saw, still wore his.

'This way,' Ashley said, and they walked quickly across the field towards a patch of wood. It was clear moonlight.

Difficult to say how long they walked. It became light, and off in the woods the birds started up.

'Here,' Ashley said, 'here it is.'

It was a clearing, quite large, and Jim thought he had been here before. And he had, he had! It was the place where he had gone with the others to collect firewood and seen the old man digging. No, not graves, but planting something. He had often thought of the man but the place itself he had forgotten, and he was surprised now to see how thick the woods were, how the blasted trees had renewed themselves with summer growth, covering their wounds, and were turning colour, now that the autumn had come, and stripping. There were thick drifts underfoot. They crackled. A few last birds were singing: two thrushes, and further off somewhere, a chaffinch. Jim moved on out of the softly slanting light. There was a garden in the clearing, neat rows of what looked like potatoes, and figures, dark-backed and slowly moving, were on their knees between the plants, digging.

He freed himself of Ashley's support, and staggered towards them. The earth smelled so good. It was a smell that belonged to the beginning of things, he could have put his nose down into it like a pig or a newly weaned calf, and the thought of filling his hands with its doughy softness was irresistible. To have dirt under his nails! Falling on his knees he began awkwardly to knead the earth, which was warm, damp, delightfully crumbly, and then to claw at it as the others were doing. It felt good.

'That's it, mate. That's the style! Dig!'

Jim looked around, astonished. It was Clancy Parkett, whom he had last seen nearly a year ago, and whom he believed was dead, blown into so many pieces that nothing of him was ever found except what Jim himself had been covered with. To give poor Clancy a decent burial, some wit had said, they would have had to bury the both of them. And now here he was quite whole after all, grinning and rasping his chin with a blackened thumb. Trust Clancy. Clancy would wriggle out of anything.

'I thought you'd been blown up,' Jim said foolishly. 'You just disappeared into thin air.'

'No,' Clancy told him, 'not air, mate. Earth.' And he held up a fistful of the richly smelling mud. 'It's the only way now. We're digging through to the other side.'

'But it'll take so long,' Jim said reasonably.

Clancy laughed. 'There's all the time in the world, mate. No trouble about time. And it's better than tryin' t' walk it.'

Jim, doubtful, began to dig. He looked about. Others were doing the same, long lines of them, and he was surprised to see how large the clearing was. It stretched away to the brightening skyline. It wasn't a clearing but a field, and more than a field, a landscape; so wide, as the early morning sun struck the furrows, that you could see the curve of the earth. There were hundreds of men, all caked with mud, long-haired, bearded, in ragged uniforms, stooped to the black earth and digging. So it must be alright after all. Why else should so many be doing it? The lines stretched out forever. He could hardly make out the last men, they were so small in the distance. And Clancy. Clancy was no fool.

He began to dig in earnest. He looked about once, seeking Ashley, but Ashley Crowther was no longer in sight.

So Jim dug along with the rest. The earth was rich and warm, it smelled of all that was good, and his back did not ache as he had expected. Nor did his knees. And there was, after all, time, however far it might be. The direct route – straight through. He looked up, meeting Clancy's humorous gaze, and they both grinned. It might be, Jim thought, what hands were intended for, this steady digging into the earth, as wings were meant for flying over the curve of the planet to another season. He knelt and dug.

18

Imogen Harcourt, still carrying her equipment – camera, plates, tripod – as she had once told Jim, 'like the implements of martyrdom,' made her way down the soft sand of the dunes towards the beach.

A clear October day.

October here was spring. Sunlight and no wind.

The sea cut channels in the beach, great Vs that were delicately ridged at the edges and ribbed within, and the sunlit rippled in them, an inch, an inch and a half of shimmering gold. Further on, the surf. High walls of water were suspended a moment, held glassily aloft, then hurled themselves forward under a shower of spindrift, a white rush that ran hissing to her boots. There were gulls, dense clouds of them hanging low over the white-caps, feeding, oystercatchers darting after crabs, crested terns. A still scene that was full of intense activity and endless change.

She set down her equipment – she didn't intend to do any work; she carried all this stuff by force of habit and because she didn't like to be separated from it, it was all she had, an extension of herself that couldn't now be relinquished. She eased the strap off her shoulder, set it all down and then sat dumpily beside it, a lone figure with her hat awry, on the white sands that stretched as far as the eye could see, all the way to the Broadwater and the southern tip of Stradbroke in one direction and in the other to Point Danger and the New South Wales border. It was all untouched. Nobody came here. Before her, where she sat with her boots dug in and her knees drawn up, was the Pacific, blue to the skyline, and beyond it, Peru.

'What am I doing here?' she asked herself, putting the question for maybe the thousandth time and finding no answer, but knowing that if she were back in Norfolk there would be the same question to be put and with no answer there either.

'I am doing' she told herself firmly, 'what those gulls are doing. Those oystercatchers. Those terns.' She pulled her old hat down hard on her curls.

The news of Jim's death had already arrived. She heard it by accident in the local store, then she heard it again from Julia Crowther, with the news that Ashley Crowther had been wounded in the same battle, though not in the same part of the field, and was convalescing in England. Then one day she ran into Jim's father.

'I lost my boy,' he told her accusingly. He had never addressed her before.

'I know,' she said. 'I'm very sorry.'

He regarded her fiercely. She had wanted to say more, to say that she understood a little of what he might feel, that for two whole days after she heard she had been unable to move; but that would have been to boast of her grief and claim for herself something she had no right to and which was too personal to be shared, though she felt, obscurely, that to share it with this man who was glaring at her so balefully and with such a deep hatred for everything he saw, might be to offer him some release from himself and to let Jim, now that he was dead, back into his life. What did he feel? What was his grief like? She couldn't tell, any more than he could have guessed at or measured hers. She said nothing. He didn't invite sympathy. It wasn't for that that he had approached her.

She sat on the beach now and watched the waves, one after another, as they rose, gathered themselves, stood poised a moment holding the sun at their crests, then toppled. There was a rhythm to it. Mathematics. It soothed, it allowed you, once you had perceived it, to breathe. Maybe she would go on from birds to waves. They were as various and as difficult to catch at their one moment.

That was it, the thought she had been reaching for. Her mind gathered and held it, on a breath, before the pull of the earth drew it apart and sent it rushing down with such energy into the flux of things. What had torn at her breast in the fact of Jim's death had been the waste of it, all those days that had been gathered towards nothing but his senseless and brutal extinction. Her pain lay in the acute vision she had had of his sitting as she had seen him on that first day, all his intense being concentrated on the picture she had taken of the sandpiper, holding it tight in his hand, but holding it also in his eye, his mind, absorbed in the uniqueness of the small creature as the camera had caught it at just that moment, with its head cocked and its fierce alert eye, and in entering that one moment of the bird's life – the bird was gone, they might never see it again – bringing up to the moment, in her vision of him, his own being that was just then so very like the birds, alert, unique, utterly present.

It was that intense focus of his whole being, it's *me*, Jim Saddler, that struck her with grief, but was also the thing – and not simply as an image either – that endured. That in itself. Not as she might have preserved it in a shot she had never in fact taken, nor even as she had held it, for so long, as an untaken image in her head, but in itself, as it for its moment was. That is what life meant, a unique presence, and it was essential in every creature. To set anything above it, birth, position, talent even, was to deny to all but a few among the infinite millions what was common and real, and what was also, in the end, most moving. A life wasn't *for* anything. It simply was.

She watched the waves build, hang and fall, one after the other in decades, in centuries, all morning and on into the early afternoon; and was preparing, wearily, to gather up her equipment and start back – had risen in fact, and shouldered the tripod, when she saw something amazing.

A youth was walking – no, running, on the water. Moving fast over the surface. Hanging delicately balanced there with his arms raised and his knees slightly bent as if upheld by invisible strings. She had seen nothing like it. He rode rapidly towards her; then, on the crest of the wave, sharply outlined against the sky, went down fast into the darkening hollow, fell, and she saw a kind of plank flash in the sunlight and go flying up behind him.

She stood there. Fascinated. The youth, retrieving the board among the flurry of white in the shallows, knelt upon it and began paddling out against the waves. Far out, a mere dot on the sunlit water, where the waves gathered and began, she saw him paddle again, then miraculously rise, moving faster now, and the whole performance was repeated: the balance, the still dancing on the surface, the brief etching of his body against the sky at the very moment, on the wave's lip, when he would slide into its hollows and fall.

That too was an image she would hold in her mind.

Jim, she said to herself, *Jim, Jim*, and hugged her breast a little, raising her face to the light breeze that had come with afternoon, feeling it cold where the tears ran down. The youth, riding towards her, was blurred in the moment before the fall.

She took up her camera and set the strap to her shoulder. There was a groove. She turned her back to the sea and began climbing the heavy slope, where her boots sank and filled and the grains rolled away softly behind. At the top, among the pigweed that held the dunes together, she turned, and the youth was still there, his arms extended, riding.

It was new. So many things were new. Everything changed. The past would not hold and could not be held. One day soon, she might make a photograph of this new thing. To catch its moment, its brilliant balance up there, of movement and stillness, of tense energy and ease – that would be something.

This eager turning, for a moment, to the future, surprised and hurt her.

Jim, she moaned silently, somewhere deep inside. *Jim. Jim*. There was in there a mourning woman who rocked eternally back and forth; who would not be seen and was herself.

But before she fell below the crest of the dunes, while the ocean was still in view, she turned and looked again.